Raider moved on unt him in his tracks. He turned. It was Delaplane, standing spread-legged, a smoking pistol in each hand.

"Good boy, Raider. Now, hand her over."

"Like hell."

"Give her here, that's an order!" Slowly, Delaplane brought up both his six-guns.

"Order my ass, you stupid bastard!"

"Set her on the ground and back off with your hands up. I'll give you three seconds. One, two. . . ."

QUEENS OVER DEUCES

BERKLEY BOOKS, NEW YORK

QUEENS OVER DEUCES

A Berkley Book / published by arrangement with
the author

PRINTING HISTORY
Berkley edition / January 1984

ISBN: 0-425-06743-2

PRINTED IN THE UNITED STATES OF AMERICA

CHAPTER ONE

Kansas, carpeted with low-growing buffalo grass, its flatness interrupted only by distant stands of cottonwood, spread away from both sides of the stopped train. The sun, blazing down out of the cloudless blue sky, seemed to focus its fury on the vestibule of the custom-built car in which Raider and Doc stood in their sweat-dampened clothes in the sweltering, motionless air. Doc leaned against the lazytongs gate drawing undisguisable pleasure and smoke from his Old Virginia cheroot. They could hear the muffled gurgling sound of water flowing from the tank at the side of the rail bed down its hose into the boiler. Raider removed his Stetson and wiped his brow with the back of his forearm.

He was not a happy man; contentment and peace of mind were not his. Rather, his mood was disagreeable, as evidenced by the scowl on his face.

"I just think it's downright unfair for the ol' bastard to dump this load o' Mexican oats in our two laps. After all we've done for the agency, for the damn Pinkerton name, the cases we've busted, the high-line riders and killers we've collared, the money and loot we've recovered. To take his two best operatives, his two saltiest dogs, and assign 'em to baby-sit some pea-brained foreigner, his missus, and his maw don't make a lick o' sense. Tell me it does, does it? It don't, you know it don't!"

"Rade, keep it down, they'll hear you."

1

"Who the hell cares?"

"Look at the bright side. It's only for three weeks. We'll be enjoying a nice, relaxing ride across Kansas, without risking our necks; we don't even need guns this time out. We're not after anybody, nobody's after us. Good food, good accommodations . . ."

"My ass!" Raider stabbed the air with a forefinger recently broken in three places when his horse fell on his hand, rendering the digit as crooked as his partner's shrinking cheroot. "That man's mouth never stops talkin', an' never says nothin' worth the hearin'. What I'm sayin' is, that's a six-year-old playin' at bein' a grown-up, that's all that is."

"He's a king, Rade. Like all royalty he's been cloistered and coddled from the cradle. It's not his fault. Look at the bright side."

"You just said that. Man, don't you never listen when you talk?"

"Look at Queen Milena, and don't say you haven't. You can't take your eyes off her."

Raider softened his scowl, bringing the ends of his mouth up in the suggestion of a smile. The change of subject patently pleased him. He whistled low and meaningfully.

"Ain't she somethin', though? Ripe an' round in the right places, you bet. An' then some. Man, I'd give my left eye to see her with my right flat on the bed an' ready to spread. What a crotchful! What a waste. . . . I bet you she ain't let him north o' her knees since the weddin' night, which he musta messed up for fair, poor woman."

"You don't know that. Ease up on him. He's a decent sort, a gentleman."

"He's a four-square, double-rigged asshole!" Raider paused, leered, and snickered. "Speakin' o' eyeballin', I been watchin' the dow, dow . . ."

"Dowager Queen Ernestine. A dowager, Rade, is a king or nobleman's widow, one who holds some title or property."

"What she's holdin' is the hots for you, Dr. Weatherbee. She might not be much of a looker, but I bet you she knows how to shake the bed and wet the sheets."

"You are crude, Rade. Aside from which, the lady's old enough to be my mother."

"She don't look too far west o' fifty to me. She ain't exactly comin' apart at the joints." His laugh bore an undercurrent of insinuation. "Best keep your eyes open, fella. She's fixin' to make her move on you. Wouldn't surprise me none if she sneaked into our car one night an' woke you up with her throat round your bellrope."

Doc shook his head, his expression suddenly weary. "You're a marvel, Rade. Whatever the subject of conversation— innocent, sacred, or sublime—you have the most uncanny knack for filthifying it."

Raider ignored this observation. "I'll say one thing for Nick," he went on. "He sure got a good eye for hardware. Them three shotguns o' his look to be hand tooled, I mean from hinge bolts to butt plates. Did you catch that gold inlay work on the stock o' that Italian piece?"

"You mean the Bernardelli. What about the silver on the Franchi Aristocrat? Each side of the stock is a different hunting scene. It's magnificent. It must have cost a fortune."

"I bet you he can't hit the broad side of a barn from inside. The richer the dude, the better the piece, the worse the eye."

Doc drew contentedly, his full attention on the effort, setting the end of the cheroot blazing brightly, circling his lips and sending a succession of two-inch rings upward, gently assaulting the vestibule ceiling.

"I don't know, Rade. Montenegro is a mountainous country. Probably loaded with game. Besides, why come all the way to Kansas after buffalo if you don't know how to shoot? You know what your trouble with him is, you don't give him a chance. The biggest thing you dislike about him is his lady. You think she's wasted on him, and that you resent."

"You sayin' I'm jealous? O' that pasty-faced, squeaky-voiced, milk-soppin' swivel dude? Chrissakes, every time he comes into the damn car I feel like gettin' up to give him my seat! Jealous, that's a laugh! How could any man be jealous o' that? If you want to know the truth, it ain't him that bothers me half as much as the assignment. Three weeks o' this is gonna be like three weeks hangin' upside down.''

''I'm enjoying myself.''

''You would.''

Raider seethed in silence for a while, leaning out and watching the hose being detached from the boiler filler hole and swung dripping back to the water tank.

''Where is this place they come from, this Mon . . . Mon . . .''

''Montenegro.''

''Never heard of it.''

''You never heard of New York till you were twenty. Montenegro is in southeastern Europe, in the Balkan Peninsula.''

''Never heard o' that neither.''

''On the Adriatic Sea.''

''Never heard—''

''Between Bosnia and Herzegovina and the Primore, a strip of the Dalmatian littoral.''

''Forget I asked, okay, Mr. Show-off Mouth?''

A gun went off, so close by and so loud it sounded like a cannon. A second shot followed, setting the car shuddering on its tracks.

''What the hell . . .'' said Raider. He glanced out one side, then the other. ''What's he shootin' at, for chrissakes?''

''Come on.''

Doc threw open the door and in they surged, into a clerestory-ceilinged private car resplendent with Victorian elegance: enormous red plush upholstered tête-à-têtes and chairs with fringed arms and squads of tassels marching around their legs set on a red and gold scroll-designed side-to-side carpet. Cut-glass mirrors abounded, and heavy drapes framed the windows, contributing to a spectacle that dazzled the eye.

At one of the windows—raised, and with his shotgun protruding through it—sat His Royal Highness Nicholas Mirko Petrovitch, King of Montenegro, in scarlet jacket with gold epaulets, white riding breeches, and gleaming black boots, his collar open, his Adam's apple pulsing excitedly. Sighting down the barrel of his Franchi Aristocrat, he pulled off a third shot. At sight of the two intruders he pulled in his gun and rose from his chair, grinning like a mischievous schoolboy.

There was no sign of game outside, no birds, not so much as a prairie dog lifting its little head to eye them. The whistle hooted, the bell clanged, steam whooshed forth against the wheels, and the car jolted forward. Raider fell against Nicholas and the gun went off, blowing a hole in the floor between them, the shot nearly taking Raider's right foot with it. The queen and the dowager queen shrieked in bad harmony; Nicholas laughed like a maniac. Raider backed off in stunned amazement. The smoke cleared, and through the hole the rail bed and ties could be clearly seen.

"I target practice," said Nicholas amiably.

"At what, for chris—"

Doc's hand found Raider's arm, squeezing him silent before the expletive could take full form.

"At my first shot, of course." Nicholas gestured grandly at the prairie.

Doc sighed. "I think His Highness means he shot, saw where it hit, and shot to hit the same spot."

"I know what His Highness means," growled Raider between clenched teeth. "I just don't see no sense in it."

"Any sense," corrected Queen Milena.

In her lap lay an English phrase book. She was wearing her shining black hair in a braided coronet and had on a tight-fitting, long-sleeved silk dress ornamented with flowers. She beamed at Raider, the indulgent smile of a schoolmistress who had just corrected a pupil. Opposite her, sprawled on a tête-à-tête, was the dowager queen, thirty pounds overweight, with puffy, liberally powdered cheeks and chin surrounding a red puncture of a mouth. Her dark eyes always seemed to be narrowed, appraising everything and everyone they fixed on, as if, in Raider's mind, they were judging horseflesh.

Standing at the far end of the car, looking on, was Stefan, Nicholas's valet. Stefan was the only one present who had not reacted in the slightest, not even blinking when the king accidentally fired through the floor. Raider's glance drifted to

Stefan. He was a big man and a cool one, he thought, rugged-looking, and hard as a rock. Had he not known he was a gentleman's gentleman, Raider would have taken him for a torture chamber activities director.

The door opened behind Stefan and the two maids stuck their heads in, round-eyeing the gathering. One, a little blonde with skin as pink as an infant's and breasts that rivaled Queen Milena's, spied the hole in the floor, squealed, and covered her mouth.

"Your Highness," said Raider tiredly, "would you please mind keeping your guns in their cases unloaded till we spot a herd? What I mean is, keep any blood spillin' outside the car."

"The gun discharged accidentally, Mr. Raider," purred Milena.

He had a place, and she wanted him in it. Stay in your place, her eyes said, and don't question the actions or the words of your superiors. When your advice is needed you'll be asked for it. Raider got the message, resented it, but said nothing. Up to that moment he couldn't imagine his dislike for the assignment could possibly increase; he now knew better. He despised being there. Allan Pinkerton might just as well have ordered him and Doc to play security guards at his daughter Joan's wedding reception, make sure none of the guests lifted any of the silver or snuck any of the gifts out the door. It was degrading; it stunk! he mused. The next twenty days would be like twenty weeks. If only Lady Luck would smile and Nick would shoot himself trying to load one of his cannons. They'd call off the whole wingding for sure if he did.

No such luck, he thought. It was like asking for the moon when you're last in line. They had left Lawrence the day before, five cars plus caboose: this perfumed and plush palace on wheels; the royal sleeping car coupled to it; the dining car; the commissary and servants quarters sharing the next car; his and Doc's quarters, specially built in space taken from the baggage car. They had passed through Topeka, and coming up was Junction City. Beyond it lay Salina and, farther on,

Ellsworth. Beyond that they'd be into buffalo country, where the big herds roamed, more than three hundred miles from Kansas City.

King Nicholas wanted to stop every other mile to pot gophers, jack rabbits, prairie chickens, anything that moved and couldn't shoot back. Doc tactfully dissuaded him while Raider spurred his expectations, describing at length buffalo herds so huge they blackened the landscape as far as a man could see. Herds ten, fifteen miles wide, raising a cloud of dust that threatened to cover Kansas . . .

The train pulled on, cutting through the lush eastern half of the tall-grass prairie. In the distance Raider could see an occasional lone elk and once a small herd of pronghorns gathered by a stream about two miles away.

Nicholas saw nothing; he sat rapt, listening to Raider's exaggerating and Doc's lively contributions: men have seen herds as large as the state of Rhode Island; a million beasts is common where we're heading; Thomas Farnham, riding west of the Santa Fe Trail in 1839, took three days and nights to pass through a herd, so immense was it.

The king interrupted them only once, to ask a question: Would they both swear on their honors as Americans and gentlemen that all the buffalo would not be killed by the time they got there?

Doc was right in praising the accommodations on board; not even Raider, prince of pessimists and, in Billy Pinkerton's view, harder to please than a hooker at an army post, could downgrade the quality of the meals. The evening's choice of red snapper in a white wine sauce with French peas, mutton with caper sauce, or grouse Macedonian style, a veritable armada of soups and vegetables, and desserts of a richness and variety calculated to please the most fastidious palate, gave new meaning to the phrase "fit for a king." Raider drank Scotch whiskey; Doc switched back and forth between an "impertinent" Chablis and Madeira.

He retired before Raider to their small but not at all cramped sleeping quarters. Undressing and washing for bed, he appraised his image in the mirror. Dinner—as had lunch, and breakfast before it—had taken him back to the good life back east, at college and subsequently, before joining the Pinkerton National Detective Agency. From that day forward, only patches of luxury—or even ease—had been his to enjoy. It was mostly dirty and dangerous work, cold food, bad liquor, run-down hotels, hot beans and hotter coffee on the trail, and discomfort and deprivation at every turn. All the things Raider took for granted in life.

He slipped between the sheets in the raw—not his customary way of sleeping, but both sensible and desirable in the relentless heat, which even the coming of darkness failed to dispel. Two days down, nineteen to go, he mused, yawning. A vacation for the two of them, whether Raider agreed or not, a more than welcome break from their usual routine, from clashing with miscreants, living in the saddle or on the seat of the apothecary wagon that served as his cover on the move. Rubbing elbows with royalty gave one the feeling of *being* royal yourself, at least temporarily, however misguided the assumption. Only two members of the party appeared to be looking down their noses at them—Milena and Stefan. Dowager Queen Ernestine was being perfectly charming, with her pleasant laugh and motherly warmth. True, she had a way of looking *through* you, as if you were a windowpane, but she did not put either of them down as Milena was continually putting Raider down. The withering look she hung on her face when he sounded off, and her barbed rejoinders, had only one objective: to take him down a peg; to remind him who he was and who he was with.

Old Rade couldn't care less, he reflected, grinning to himself. His eyes were on things other than Milena's face, and his ears were apparently closed.

He fell asleep. The green turtle soup mingling with the mutton, mince pie, and Madeira set him to dreaming. He was in the royal bedchamber, in a capacious bed as soft as a cloud. Its posts supported a canopy inscribed with the coat of arms of the Royal House of Weatherbee. The other furnishings were equally sumptuous. The door opened and in stepped his queen, looking very much like Maria, Queen Ernestine's petite blond lady-in-waiting/maid. She smiled, struck a fetching pose, and ran the tip of her tongue sensuously back and forth over her glistening upper lip. She wore a scarlet and beige silk peignoir. She undid the sash as she glided forward, letting the peignoir drop from her shoulders, revealing her stark naked, her large, full breasts high and wantonly aggressive, their reddish-brown nipples as hard as nailheads. Approaching the bed, she threw aside the coverlet and, sinking to her knees, dropped her luscious mouth down onto his cock, sucking it gently. Under assault by her tongue, suddenly wildly thrashing, his cock began hardening, rising, swelling, and throbbing like the head of a drum beaten in rhythm. He could feel come silently rumbling in his balls. Back and forth between cheeks she sent the firm, red head of his cock, while her swollen tongue lashed and laved it lovingly. Then down her throat it went, sucked deep, her quivering lips circling and seizing the base of it, working the head against the wet walls of her throat. He came, his load exploding, filling her mouth. She swallowed and swallowed. . . .

He woke to discover a familiar face poised above his spent member. Queen Ernestine's fat pink tongue was out, the tip of it wiping stray gobs of come from around her mouth, a satisfied smile widening it, raising her plump cheeks and filling her eyes with a slightly glazed look.

"My God!" blurted Doc hoarsely.

"You did not enjoy it?" she asked. She looked confused, even disappointed.

"I . . . I . . ."

"Let us start over again. I will do it differently this time. You will adore this way; I promise."

Doc groaned, swallowed the lump in his throat painfully, and, leaning his head back on his pillow, slowly closed his eyes.

The train had stopped—just in time to avoid a derailment. The engineer had sighted a dislodged rail ahead and applied the brakes. The three-man crew was now busy restoring the rail. The royal party had deserted the parlor car, all but Queen

Milena, who, with Raider, lingered over coffee. That is, the tall, swarthy, and temperamental Pinkerton lingered, at the behest of the queen. He was tired and he wanted bed, but he hesitated to say so for fear of insulting the lady.

"I am curious," she purred, "so you must permit me to pry. How long have you been a detective?"

"The agency calls us operatives; it's the same difference. About thirteen months now."

"And have you killed many men?"

"Sure."

"How many?"

"Six hundred fifty-three."

She gasped. "Surely you joke!"

"Surely I do."

They sipped their coffee. He stifled a yawn and excused himself. She smiled alluringly. God, she was beautiful, he thought, just picture-perfect—every feature, every hair in place, skin like lilies, with the faintest blush to her cheeks. She had a way of tilting her head slightly to one side when she was listening, studying him out of the corners of her fantastic green eyes filled with a smoldering look that set him to swallowing so he couldn't stop. God, she was beautiful.

Once again she sipped. He did also.

"Is there much danger . . . from the criminals and the red men?"

"Anytime guns start goin' off it can get touchy. You saw what happened to the floor."

"What has been your most dangerous assignment?"

He was staring at her ring, a white crown set in a large ruby with the letters H and I on either side.

"That is the royal seal of Montenegro."

"It's sure pretty."

"You were saying, your most dangerous case . . ."

"There've been a few hairy ones."

"Hairy?"

"Would you mind if we changed the subject, Your Highness?"

"You may call me Milena . . . when we are just the two of us like this."

"I'm 'fraid I wouldn' feel comfortable, you bein' what you are, an' me bein' . . ."

"What?"

"What I am."

"I think you are a very courageous man. To risk your life in your job . . . What is the attraction? Is it glory?"

Her voice seemed to fade, as if someone or something was pushing her away speedily. In seconds they were so far apart he could barely hear her.

"It cannot be the money. It must be the glory, the adventure. Are you married?"

He opened his mouth to respond, his eyes rolled up in his head, his face fell forward. The last thing he remembered was a sharp pain as he smashed the area around his nose against the rim of his empty cup.

CHAPTER TWO

Raider's skull had been split into halves; this was the first certainty that shaped itself in his mind upon awakening. The second was that the wall beside the bed was toppling down on him. He raised his arm to keep it from falling. The suddenness of the movement sent a wide wedge of pain through the space between the halves of his skull, piercing his exposed brain and sending great freshets of blood spurting in every direction, washing down his eyes, blinding him redly.

"Sweet Jesus Christ."

Speaking sent a second wedge of pain after the first.

"You are awake. How wonderful!"

The voice was tinged with sarcasm. But it wasn't the sarcasm, it was the voice that iced up his spine. Her Royal Highness Queen Milena of Montenegro leaned over him and leered. He noticed that she was as naked as a newly hatched jay, one massive breast pressing warmly and hard against his rib cage. He too was naked. Some instinct born of his wide experience with women urged him to check his jewels. Glancing down through the thicket on his chest, down the plane of his belly to his crotch, he could see his cock. As red, swollen, and abused-looking as a rooster's after a sweep through the henhouse.

He sighed.

"What is the matter, my love?"

He lowered his arm, confident that the wall would stay up. Finding his head with both hands, he rubbed it tentatively.

"Lady," he murmured, "what in red hell did you put in my coffee, dynamite?"

She giggled. "A sleeping potion. It's perfectly harmless; I use it myself frequently."

"How long have I been out?"

"Two days."

He jerked up to a sitting position, instantly regretting it. "Ahhhhh . . ."

"Does your head hurt?"

"It feels like somebody dropped a twenty-pound Vulcan anvil on it."

She got out of bed. "I will get you a damp cloth. You will feel better in no time. You will see. I'll be your angel of mercy. I shall take splendid care of you."

He placed the flat of his hand over his jewels. Damn, his cock was sore!

"Feels like you already have."

She laughed airily. In the other room he could hear her dipping a washcloth into the water basin and wringing it out. Pulling the sheet up to his navel, he glanced about the room. It looked clean and was freshly painted. There were none of the familiar odors generally associated with hotel rooms: ammonia, vomit, bay rum, or mustiness. She came back, her thighs framing the blackest snatch he had ever seen. And the most beautiful; he sensed his mouth watering. Kneeling on the bed, she laid the cloth across his forehead. Then she got up and put on her robe. She stood before the mirror, running a comb through her long hair, humming contentedly to herself. Had he fucked her, he wondered? How could he, unconscious? On second thought, he could; rather, she could do all the necessaries—the preparation and positioning.

"How could I be out two whole days?" he asked. "They don't make knockout drops can put a man out that long."

"Two days," she said flatly, in the imperious tone he had come to know and respect. "You must be hungry, starving."

"Where are we?"

"Pawnee City."

"Nebraska? That's crazy, that's a hundred miles from where we stopped. You're all mixed up. What did we do, fly?"

She crossed to the door and took down the sign from the back of it. She handed it to him.

"Look at the bottom."

He mumbled to himself: "J. B. Heathercott, Manager, Pawnee House, Pawnee City, Neb— Man, you really are crazy. Stark, staring! You got any idea what you've gone an' did?"

"Done."

"Your husband's gonna think I kidnapped you, not t'other way round. Hell no! Me, I did it! He's gonna come after us, after me with the whole damn Omaha barracks, with the damn Division o' the Missouri, Tecumsah Sherman, an' Phil Sheridan both. They'll catch me, they'll hang me! Christ Jesus, Allan Pinkerton'll hang me, President Grant'll hang me, everybody. They'll have to draw lots! Woman, you are crazier than a bedbug with a tick on it, you got to be!"

One hand holding his head securely to his neck, he scrambled out of bed. Weaving and groaning about the room like a drunk, he got into his clothes, then he vanished into the other room to dash water on his face. His ablutions completed, he marched to the door, unlocked it, and jerked it wide. He turned to her.

"Thanks for nothin'!"

Turning to exit, he came face to chest with a man tall and wide enough to all but entirely fill the doorway. Only the spaces above his shoulders showed light. His arms were folded, his jaw—half the size of a building block—jutted forward belligerently. His face was that of a bull terrier minus the blackness around the nose and the two eyeteeth thrusting upward from the lower jaw. Nor did his ears hang down over their apertures. But the resemblance between man and beast was uncanny. Raider swallowed and sighed.

"Kindly step aside, friend."

The dog-man stood fast and leered. Once more Raider

sighed. Half turning, he drew back his right hand and rammed his fist into the other man's brisket with all the force he could muster.

"Owwwwwww!"

Roaring, he shook his hand violently. Again the man leered. A thought whipped through Raider's mind. Two steps back, lower his head, and charge the bastard. No. Wrong head for the job.

"Your Highness, will you please tell your friend here to unblock the doorway?"

"I cannot do that, Raider."

Even as she answered, Raider was closing on the brute. Shaking his sore fist under his nose to distract him, he brought his right knee up as high as he could and slammed his heel down as hard as he could. The man howled in pain and began dancing on one foot, seizing the other with his shovel-sized hands. Raider brushed by him, swinging right.

There stood a second obstacle just as huge, just as menacing-looking. Flinging his hands up in surrender, Raider went back into the room. Milena came swishing by him, closing and relocking the door.

"I can't leave you," he said quietly. "You already got me in the deep soup. Leaving you to go back an' try to explain would really tear it. No, you an' me got to go back together, an' pronto."

She stood facing him, her hands on her hips, her sensuous lips pursed thoughtfully, her lovely eyes dancing. A smile slowly lit up her beautiful face. She began shaking her head from side to side.

CHAPTER THREE

King Nicholas sat with his Franchi Aristocrat across his lap, gazing out the window at the prairie, which was briefly bronzed by the setting sun. Doc, seated opposite him, marveled at his aplomb. The man had buffalo on the brain, he reflected, with no room in his thinking for the catastrophe that had tumbled into his regal lap. His valet Stefan was not nearly so poised; nor was Queen Ernestine. Or the two Secret Service men who had boarded the train in Junction City in response to the message tapped out by the trainman at Ernestine's urging. The two newcomers looked like a vaudeville team. One was a head and a half taller than his partner, supporting a flowing handlebar mustache that overwhelmed his slender face and made his skinny neck look even skinnier. The other's physique resembled a barrel with a globe perched atop it. He had no neck, no shoulders; his most distinctive feature was his voice, which seemed to rise all the way up from the bottom of the barrel, carrying with it an authority that severely contradicted his appearance. Comical though they may have looked to Doc, both gave the impression of knowing how to go about their work.

"Your principal, Mr. Pinkerton, has been alerted," said Gillespie, the taller of the two.

Doc groaned inwardly. This news came as no surprise, but that didn't make it any easier to accept.

"Let's go over the whole thing from start to finish one

more time," suggested Harrigan, Gillespie's partner. "Number one, all of you were asleep from midnight on, right?" Heads, all save Nicholas's, nodded, his mind and his hearing being elsewhere. "Which means the kidnapping had to take place sometime between the hours of twelve and six."

"Hold it," interposed Doc. "You seem to take it for granted that Raider kidnapped Her Highness. It's just possible it could be the other way around, you know."

"I seriously doubt that," said Gillespie, his tone overbearing. "I think you do too, if you want to be honest. When was the last time you heard of a woman kidnapping a man? No go, it just isn't possible, fellow."

"In this instance it's very possible, 'fellow.' "

Stefan glared at Doc. Nicholas had turned from the window and was eyeing him curiously. Ernestine's expression was noncommittal. Both maids continued their gaping. The incident was all too obviously titillating to the two of them. They were seizing on every word with the eagerness of a starving dog going for a bone.

"That is a most offensive and slanderous remark," growled Stefan. "Men have been challenged to duel for lesser insults."

"Oh, shut up," said Doc.

Stefan bristled. "What did you say? Would you mind repeating that? Do you dare to?"

Suddenly glowering, he took a step toward Doc. Gillespie stepped between them. Nicholas laughed quietly, drawing everyone's attention.

"Cut it out, you two," said Gillespie. "Let's not get off the track. Go on, Paul."

Harrigan continued, his eyes riveted to Doc. "Raider did the abducting. The question is how. Obviously, with help. The derailment made it necessary to stop the train for . . . what?"

"Fifty-three minutes," said the trainman, standing with his back to the door and consulting his notebook.

"Now," continued Harrigan, "we know that somebody was waiting with a rig of some kind. We found wagon tracks near the baggage car. So, he evidently got her into the car on some pretext, knocked her out, probably with chloroform, and away they went with his confederate. Probably more than one. The tracks lead northwest in the direction of Manhattan.''

"We've already checked," went on Gillespie. "Nobody matching their descriptions has been seen up there. Of course, that doesn't mean beans. Manhattan's a fair-sized town. Folks don't pay much attention to strangers passing through. Okay, where are we? We know the direction they took starting out, but the tracks get lost in the dust, so there's no way of telling where they're headed. Every lawman in Kansas, Nebraska, Missouri, and Oklahoma has been alerted, thanks to the miracle of telegraphy.''

Doc shook his head and concentrated on the scrollwork on the carpet. He thought about Harrington and Hart at the Third Vanities Theater in New Orleans. These two weren't nearly as funny, weren't funny at all, but they were closing in fast on the ridiculous. Rade would never do such a thing under any circumstances, no matter how great the temptation. And the lady certainly was tempting. But the plowboy was without doubt the most thoroughly honorable man Doc had ever met; he wouldn't steal a toothpick, let alone a queen.

His eyes drifted to Nicholas, who continued to hang on to his expensive shotgun like a small boy to his favorite toy. He was scanning the darkening landscape. He spotted something, raised the window, and fired, missing a jackrabbit by three feet.

"The devil!" he snapped.

Clearly, he did not miss his wife, nor was his male ego bruised in the slightest by the incident. Doc wondered if he loved Milena. It could be he was incapable of loving any woman. Raider could be right: The man was an imperial disaster in bed. To a woman as sensual as Milena, a woman who needed all the sex she could get and could well handle it, Nicholas must be the blight of her life. He knew it, and he couldn't care less.

Everybody else cared, except Ernestine. Oh, she cared all right, he mused; she was enjoying every minute of this. Apart from arousing a dormant streak of romance in her, it placed her lovely daughter-in-law in a very bad light. To be enjoyed by another man. A commoner. A foreigner. Whether it was Milena's fault or not, it wasn't going to do her any good. Not to her mother-in-law's way of thinking.

Where had she taken Rade? How was he handling it? He'd bring her back first chance he got, fully prepared to face the music. If and when he did bring her back it would have to be over her objections. Which meant she'd be certain to get even with him by heaping all the blame on his shoulders. Poor Rade. Allan Pinkerton would beat him to death with a chair leg. President Grant would stand him in front of a whole succession of firing squads. The thing had all the makings of an international incident. Thank God it was little Montenegro they came from, and not England or France. Either of them and they might declare war.

"Poor Rade," he said.

"What was that?" asked Harrigan.

"Nothing."

Gillespie turned to the trainman, an aged, balding individual with a homely face that hung from his skull like loose pie dough.

"We've been sitting here long enough. The last orders we had from Kansas City were to get back there. Our chief, Colonel Worthington Pryor, and Mr. Pinkerton will have arrived by the time we get there."

"*No!*"

Everyone reacted startled. Nicholas was on his feet, scowling. "We cannot go back. We have come here to shoot the buffalo, and by the devil, I will shoot him."

"But, Your Highness—" began Stefan.

The king silenced him with a wave. "She can wait. She's not going anyplace. Once she gets into bed she will stay there. She can stay in bed for days." His eyes traveled from face to face. "She's not leaving the country. No, we will not return to Kansas City. You, trainman, tell the engineer to start the train. We will go on to where the buffalo are. Stefan, bring me my other two guns. I must be prepared for when we arrive.'' He beamed proudly. "I can see in the dark like a cat.''

"Don't be a ninny, Nicky," said his mother. "We have to go back. These men have to find her. It's bad enough already. How do you think this will make you look in the newspapers? And to compound it by ignoring it, going on to shoot your foolish buffalo . . .''

"The buffalo is not foolish, Mama. It is a magnificent beast. Dr. Weatherbee said so. Didn't you, Dr. Weatherbee?''

"Nicky, be quiet. Do not interrupt your mama." She nodded to Gillespie and Harrigan in turn. "We will do as you say. We will return to Kansas City.''

"Mama . . .''

"We will go back and hunt for the little hussy. And when we find her and we're all back together again, we can come back and you can shoot all the buffalo you please.''

"Promise? Cross your heart? Swear by St. Basil? Swear, swear . . .''

His mother obliged. Doc shook his head and resumed studying the scrollwork in the carpet. There was nothing particularly unusual about it. The contrast in colors, gold on vermilion, was undeniably attractive, but the design itself was quite common. His attention drifted to the small throw rug put down by the trainman over the hole in the floor, testimony to Nicholas's marksmanship. Reflecting on the incident, and dismissing it, his thoughts went back to the previous night and his visitor. Queen Ernestine. She, not Gillespie or Harrigan, was in charge, with her son securely wrapped around her little finger. And right beside him was Doc Weatherbee—just as Raider was now wrapped around Queen Milena's little finger.

Queens over deuces . . .

CHAPTER FOUR

Three days had passed in the room, the three longest, most difficult, most demanding and downright painful days of Raider's life. At Milena's suggestion he sent Bela downstairs for a plunge bath and water. She had brought along all sorts of toiletries: colognes and perfumes, bath and body powders. As far as Raider could see, the only thing she'd neglected to pack was her modesty. Taking her bath in full view of him, she put on a memorable exhibition, ignoring him completely as she washed and rinsed and otherwise attended to her most private areas.

Lying in bed, trying not to watch her and failing utterly, he could feel his sore and reddened member stiffen, fill with steel and craving, raising the sheet. She stood up, sending slender cascades of soapy water spilling down her gleaming pink body.

"Come and wash me where I cannot reach," she ordered.

"You can reach. Try real hard."

"Do as I tell you. Or would you prefer I get Bela in here to do it?"

"Which one is he?"

"The bigger one. The other is Karel. They are cousins from Mount Lovchen, near Cettigne. They were woodsmen before they came into my employ at court. Both are very strong."

"I believe you."

"And very loyal to their queen. They would kill for me."

"Is that supposed to be a warning?"

She dismissed this with a toss of her head. "Do not worry, you are perfectly safe with me. I would not permit you to be harmed. I am too fond of you. Come . . ."

He got out of bed. Earlier, when his exit had been blocked by Bela and she had relocked the door, she had taken him back to bed and fucked him for two solid hours. He was finally able to unfasten himself from her before his heart gave out only by subterfuge. Summoning every ounce of willpower at his command, he mutely ordered his tortured cock to soften and stay soft.

Now it was stiffening again, and no amount of persuasion or threatening seemed able to reverse the process.

"Come," she repeated.

He went to her. Dropping to her knees in the tub, sending sheets of water flying forth from either side and dashing on the floor, she took his cock in her mouth and began sucking it. She grabbed his ass cheeks with both hands and moved his manhood slowly in and out of the fire in her face. He could feel her tongue swell. It thrashed about like a stricken snake as she gradually tightened her lips along his shaft. It felt as if he were fucking a slowly shrinking keyhole. He wanted to pull free, but her grip on his cheeks was too strong. He finally grabbed her by the head, bending his body to remove himself, but she tightened her grip on his cheeks and sank her teeth into his joint.

"Owwwwww! Christ Jesus!"

"Do not touch my head. Just come. I want you to come. It's sweet. It's warm and delicious. Come."

He came, spurting down her throat. A gob slipped from the corner of her mouth. She caught it easily with the tip of her tongue.

"Yum, yum, yum. Now wash me. No, I shall wash you. Empty out the water and pour in the other two buckets. Hurry, I want to wash you."

By the time she was done abusing him, his cock felt as if it was ready to drop off, his nuts felt like two Christmas tree balls—hollow, fallen from their branches, and shattered on the floor. The rest of him felt as if he had dropped ten pounds along with his nuts. His crotch was on fire with pain. She dried him off briskly.

"Now let us get back into bed and do more locking."

"Please, I don't think I can even walk that far." He paused. "Lockin'?"

"Locking. You lock yourself to me. That is what we call it in my country. What do they call it in America?"

"Locking, only when they spell it the first two letters are different. Look, give me an' mine a break for a spell, can't you? I'd like to go out an' get some fresh air, a razor, a toothbrush, maybe a bottle. You came away ready for travel. All I brought was my clothes."

"Make a list of whatever you need. We will send Karel to the shops."

"Come on. Look, if you're worried about me cuttin' out, you needn't. The last thing I want to do is lose you."

She leered impishly. "You are enjoying yourself, no?"

"It's bad enough you pulled this crazy stunt. The only thing worse would be for us to split up."

She studied his eyes. "You plan to trick me and bring me back to Nicky. Do not try. You will only regret it. I have planned this too carefully, and successfully. Understand one thing: There is no power on earth that can make me go back."

"You fixin' to keep runnin' for the next ten years?"

"If necessary. I have plenty of money, I have Bela and Karel, I have you. What is there to go back for?"

He shrugged. "It's your funeral." And mine, he thought drearily. "Look, I really do want to get out for half an hour. I won't cut an' run. It wouldn't make a lick o' sense. You can see that. If you like, one o' those two overgrown lumber rustlers can come with me."

She considered this. "Very well. Karel will go along."

She opened her drawstring bag on the nightstand, taking out a roll of bills as big as his fist. He gaped. She peeled off three tens.

"Is that enough? I have plenty—more than four thousand dollars."

"What'd you do, knock over Wells Fargo?"

"I am a meticulous planner. I know exactly what I am doing every step of the way."

He began to get dressed. She sat on the bed in her peignoir, her knees drawn up, the top of the garment gaping, revealing one magnificent shiny pink breast.

"How long you been plannin' this?"

"I started the week before our ship left Antivari. Karel and Bela left on another ship the same day under explicit orders. As you can see, they carried them out to the letter. When you and your friend came aboard the train in Lawrence I decided to take you along with me."

"That was real thoughtful o' you."

She laughed. "You are enjoying every minute, do not say you are not."

"What I'll say is this: You're havin' your fun now, but it can't go on forever. Sooner or later you're gonna wind up payin' the piper. They'll find us, they'll fetch us back."

"They won't find us. We won't be staying in any one place long enough. Tomorrow we are leaving here."

"For where?"

"You will know when we get there."

She got up, went to the door, and unlocked it. As if he had been reading her mind, or listening at the keyhole, reflected Raider, Karel stood waiting. She spoke to him briefly, commandingly, in a gutteral tongue. He nodded and took Raider by the arm. Raider shook it off.

"Does this boy savvy English?" he asked.

"Not a syllable. Use sign language. You will get along all right. Do not be too long, my lover. I shall get dressed. We'll be eating out tonight."

Kissing him on the cheek, she pushed him out the door.

Raider had his new Peacemaker and a belt full of cartridges, but apart from the clothes on his back, his operative I.D. card, and four paper dollars added to Milena's three tens, that was all he was carrying. He walked down the stairs ahead of the hulking Karel, who looked like Bela only not quite as bulldog-like. Raider put him at six foot two and around 210 pounds, with a chest like a stallion, arms like city fireplugs, and not a pinch of fat on his entire frame. Walking through the dimly lit lobby, his mind reached for ideas: Pull a fast one on the big ox, dodge down the first alley, maybe trip him first, starting out with a healthy kick in the shin, then the trip, tangle him up in pain for ten seconds' head start. Or draw on the big ox and disarm him. He carried a toy about the size of Doc's .38 Diamondback jammed in his belt. Or maybe somehow get behind him and tap him on the skull with his gun butt.

Then what? Steal a horse and get back to the train. Where was it about now? Not sitting where they'd left it. No doubt gone back to Lawrence, maybe even Kansas City. He and Doc had boarded in Lawrence, but the train had been assembled and the royal party had gotten on in Kansas City. Yes, they'd gone back, without Nicky getting so much as a single buffalo in his sights. He must be steaming!

The chief would be sticking his oar in by now, and the Secret Service, and the ambassador to Montenegro, and their ambassador to the United States. President Grant, the Army, the Navy, every lawman west of Pittsburgh. What a mess. . . .

They reached the street. It was late afternoon, and the sun was sitting on the top of a feed and grain warehouse to their right. Pawnee City claimed a population of around four hundred. Few people were out. Opposite the hotel he spotted the Western Union office. Through the window he could see a man in his shirt-sleeves, wearing a green eyeshade, sitting at a desk over his work. Raider half turned to look back at Karel, who was three steps behind. Wouldn't it be great if he could ditch the big ox for five minutes, just long enough to run over and get off a wire to Doc in Kansas City. The same one to Lawrence, too, to be safe. Let him know where they'd gotten to and that Queen Milena was okay. Okay? She was diamonds, the crazy bitch! Too bad he couldn't tell Doc where they were heading. When they got there they'd have three hundred bluebellies waiting for them with a brass band!

Oh yes, Karel had to go, if only just to put out his light for five little minutes. Karel tapped him on the shoulder and urged him ahead. Raider sighed and walked on down the street. Maybe on the way back, he thought.

They passed Lenox's Drug Store. The windows were plastered with signs advertising Faith Whitcomb's Nerve Bitters and Whitcomb's Remedy. Was Whitcomb one of the family, he wondered? A thought struck him. He turned back, pointing.

"We'll go in here. I need toothwash."

He pantomimed brushing his teeth. Karel frowned and nodded.

Inside, Raider spotted what he wanted almost immediately.

"Give me a bottle o' that chloroform," he said to the slender, ancient, and rawhide-tough-looking man behind the counter. He laid down one of the bills Milena had given him, got his purchase wrapped in butcher's paper, took his change, and left.

He bought a razor, a brush, a toothbrush—the first one he had ever owned. They stopped off at a saloon and he invested in two quarts of Passamore County Rye Whiskey—"America's Finest." They were on their way back, within sight of the Pawnee House, with a long, narrow, dark, and inviting alley coming up on their right, which Raider had spotted when they'd passed it earlier, when a group of people came boiling out of the hotel and into a waiting stage.

"Jesus Christ!" roared Raider.

They were three men and a woman, unmistakably Milena! The door slammed shut, one of the men pulled himself up top, the driver sitting waiting snapped his whip, and off went the four mares sharing the singletree.

Raider and Karel ran after them, firing their weapons. The coach careened around a corner and was gone. On ran Raider, cursing loudly, leaving Karel farther and farther behind. The ox was big, the ox was strong, but he couldn't run worth a lick. Around the corner and into a narrow street leading out of town ran Raider, past a mustang tethered to a hitching rack, swishing its tail contentedly. Freeing the reins, he vaulted into the saddle, dropping his bag and smashing the two bottles.

"Goddamn son of a bitch!"

He rode off, hammering the horse's ribs with his heels, flattening in the saddle, getting off the last slug in the chamber, trying for and missing the driver up top. Gripping the mustang's ribs with his legs, he fumbled one cartridge after another out of his belt, reloaded, and dropped two shells as he did so, accompanying their loss with curses.

The stage was a good quarter mile ahead, but he was moving twice as fast and closing the gap . . . until a shot whistled by his right ear, and a second plowed through the crown of his Stetson. He ducked lower. A third shot, from a Winchester wielded by the man sitting alongside the driver, whizzed past his hat brim. The coach was slowing. He slowed.

"Hol' it right thar!" snapped the Winchester up on his feet. "Best come on no further."

"You go to hell, Buster-Bob!"

"You do an' she gets it, right through her purty royal haid!"

Milena showed her face, dark with fear. A man leaned out the same window, the muzzle of his pistol flush against her temple.

"Now, swing roun' an' move on out afore I blows your haid off. *Move!*"

In punctuation came four shots, neatly bracketing man and mustang. Raider stopped short, swung about, and started back. A melancholy thought crossed his mind. He nodded agreement.

"Yes, sir, whoever said things have got so bad they can't get any worse got to be fulla cow-barn carpetin'."

CHAPTER FIVE

The upstairs rear room in the Sunflower Hotel in Kansas City was a gloomy, sparsely furnished, single-windowed box. It was small and getting smaller by the minute, so filled with tension was it. The man sitting opposite Doc wore a full beard that was jet black with traces of gray. Under his broad forehead his deep-set eyes gleamed with fury.

The two had been arguing heatedly. Doc had gotten red in the face, and his companion had been enraged—pounding the table, stabbing the air with his finger, all but shattering the little window with his bellowing. He was quiet now, his temper reined, but he continued to seethe.

Doc had never before noticed how big Allan Pinkerton's fists were. He had been a cooper prior to becoming a private investigator. His hands looked powerful enough to bend a shotgun barrel or simultaneously snap two necks supporting two offending faces. Doc swallowed, hoping as he did so that Pinkerton would not notice.

"Weatherbee," said his superior through clenched teeth, "I'm not a mule nor a domn fool, though you may think me both. You doon't hov to coonvince me thot Raider didn't kidnop the lady. My reason for being irate is thot he failed to prevent this fiascoo. Any trained ooperative who lets himself becoome a pawn in the game, os helpless os a wee bairn, is os guilty, os blamewoorthy os if he ongineered it personally."

"I disagree—"

28

Down came one sledge hand disguised as a fist, rattling the table. "Domn it, mon, hold your bloody tongue while I speak!"

"You're branding him guilty because he failed to prevent it. How could he stop it if he was out cold?"

"You know for sairtain thot he was?"

"How else could they remove him?"

"They?"

"She didn't do it alone."

Pinkerton glared, letting this sink in. He pursed his lips and narrowed his eyes. Getting up, he began pacing, his hands behind his back, his derby tilted back.

"Three days, ond not a whisper froom him. Froom either oov thom."

"Obviously because he can't get to a telegraph office. He's probably bound and gagged."

"Poosibly."

"What else could it be?"

"What it is, what it coould be, doesn't intorest me a particle coompared to getting the two oov thom bock ond thot os speedily os poosible. This may not be the biggest nor the moost impoortant case we've ever hod, boot it is far ond away the moost omborrossing."

He stopped pacing and, taking a telegram out of his pocket, handed it to Doc. It was from the President. It was clear and to the point. With a vengeance. "Unconditional Surrender" Grant was holding the Pinkerton National Detective Agency completely responsible, and Chief Allan Pinkerton personally responsible "in this unfortunate and most embarrassing situation."

"The coals are oon my head, Weatherbee. Every hoor thot goes by sees the agency's reputation further besmirched. Oor good name is being held oop to ridicule. The newspapers are pillorying oos. Keep one thing oopermoost in mind: We weren't ossigned to the case ofter the foct. We—you two— were there, supposedly doing your dooty, guarding thot boonch. Ond right oonder your nooses—"

"I know, I know."

"What were you doing whon they fled the scene?"

"Sleeping, what do you think? You talked to Gillespie. It happened sometime between midnight and six in the morning. I was in my berth in the baggage car."

"Not a soul oon board so mooch os soospected they'd fled oontil soonup. Whoever plonned the thing knew whot he was aboot."

"She—"

"We're oop ogainst a blonk wall for fair. There's naught we con do boot sit aroond ond twiddle oor thombs oontil word coomes froom Raider. Which may never hoppen. We con't start looking. We've not the faintest idea where to begin."

"Every lawman in the Midwest is looking."

"This is not every lawmon's job." Snatching the wire back, he snapped his finger against it. "They've made oos respoonsible for finding her. Ond rightly so"—he pushed his knuckles down on the table and leaned over Doc, his lips two inches from his ear—"seeing os we're the ones who lost her." He straightened and fastened his eyes on him. "Enoough shilly-shallying. It's past time you went to work. Whot's your plon?"

"I don't have one. Why don't we start with a crystal ball?"

"Spare me the sarcasm."

"Spare me the abuse. The first thing we do is obvious."

"Distribute doodgers oov Her Royal Highness accoompanied by a sootible reward. Twenty-five thoosand is a healthy figure. Her picture is in oll the papers. Raider's, too."

"A reward might at least get us some leads. If we could only get on their tracks. They've got to be on the move."

"Domn ond dooble domn the papers! Everyone colls Raider her abdoocter. You don't suppose . . ." He paused. His eyes suddenly held a guilty look.

"I do not! *He's* the victim, not her. He'd be the last man on earth to do such a thing. And I resent your even suggesting it! And when he does get back and you haul him on the carpet, don't make the stupid mistake of accusing him. You do, and I promise you—''

''Enoough! Your loyalty is tooching, but I'm not accostomed to being oddressed in soch a monner. Hooever, oonder the present circoomstonces, I shall ignore it.''

''Don't. I want you to remember every word I'm saying.''

Pinkerton bristled and was about to snap back when a light tapping sounded at the door.

''Yes?''

It opened, revealing Queen Ernestine. She beamed at Doc. ''Excuse me, gentlemen.''

''Coom in, coom in, Your Highness. Operative Weatherbee ond I wore joost finishing oop.''

''How nice, then you don't mind if I steal him from you?''

A rare grin broadened Pinkerton's face. ''Noot ot oll.''

''Chief . . .''

''Go along with Her Highness, Weatherbee, I'll tend to the preporations we discoosed. Joost send oop those two Secret Sorvice lods. We moost keep thom ooprised.''

Doc nodded and followed a bubbling and delighted Ernestine out like a just-thrashed hound trailing its master. He knew when he was licked.

Raider deserted the road and started in a wide circle. He was determined to continue the pursuit, but only at a safe distance. He was puzzled. Mr. Winchester had him in his sights and could easily have blown him back to town, but he'd been careful not to. He groaned aloud. Being killed wasn't such a bad idea. At least he'd be able to say good-bye to the aggravation afflicting his crotch, which was becoming more painful with every jounce and bounce. Rising, he rode straight-legged six inches up from the saddle through a rugged hilly area that was patched with coarse grass and weeds. The kidnappers were moving in a northwesterly direction, heading toward Beatrice, the Big Blue River, and the sandhills country beyond.

He was now a good mile behind them and could no longer actually see the stage, only the fat dust pillar sent up by the rear wheels. Nightfall was still three hours ahead. The moon was in its first quarter. He could smell rain in the air. With a little luck the sky would be overcast, hiding the stars, deepening the darkness. He'd be able to get closer without their spotting him. If they did, he'd be a dead man. He'd had his first and last warning.

Why didn't Winchester shoot him when he had the chance, he wondered? The answer came to him: Kill him and nobody would be left to tell the law what had happened to Milena. Not Bela or Karel; they'd be long gone by now. Assigned to guard their queen, entrusted with the care and keeping of her royal person, had to be the biggest responsibility they'd ever been handed. And they'd botched it miserably.

The four who had horned in had to be after a ransom. They'd read the newspapers and recognized their golden chance. The desk clerk must have been in cahoots with them.

He had to give the bastards credit for one thing: They sure didn't let any grama grow under their feet. Yes, him they'd let live, probably figuring he'd run to the law for help first chance he got. Then, when they got around to demanding their money, Nicholas and Ernestine and everybody with a badge would know they really were holding Milena.

Bastards. He had about as much fondness for her as he could fit under his thumbnail. She was mouthy and demanding, and she treated him like a damn lapdog, the way she treated Nicholas and every other man. But he sure didn't want her harmed. Not as long as he was looking out for her. Some looking out! Three days and he hadn't done a damn thing right yet.

The wind came up, lifting a sheet of sand from a bare spot and whipping him in the face with it. The mustang shared the abuse and whinnied in annoyance. On he rode through the gathering gloom, well off the road, keeping the dust pillar at the corner of his right eye, weighing and reweighing his chances of kidnapping her from her kidnappers without putting her in any more danger than she was already. From where he sat, considering all aspects of the thing, it looked about as possible as finding gold in his hat.

Maybe they'd stop in Rockford, before Beatrice, someplace, anyplace big enough for a telegraph office. Give him five minutes, he'd get the whole sorry story off to Doc, give him a rough idea where they were heading, and he could organize a reception like old home week.

He was kidding himself. They weren't about to stop. Certainly not this early on. They must figure he was still on their tail. Keep going and he wouldn't have a chance to stop, wouldn't dare for fear of losing them. When they did pull up to stretch their legs, to feed and water the horses, it would likely be someplace out at the edge of hell and gone.

They appeared to be heading for a hideout. If they kept going all night and crossed the Platte, they'd be into the sand hills and sparse country.

He followed three quarters of a mile behind them for two hours. Darkness settled over Nebraska. The stars appeared, pulsing insolently at him. Reviling the absence of overcast and the continuation of his rotten luck, he nevertheless closed the distance separating them. They skirted Rockford and took a right fork, heading north for Filley. On and on they rolled. He was getting hungry. They must be too, he thought, unless they'd packed food with them. Why wouldn't they? They seemed to be prepared for everything; everything they'd done so far had been according to plan. He wondered how they had taken Bela, on guard outside Milena's door. He was about as bright as a stove lid. One of them could have decoyed him while another snuck up behind and cold-cocked him. Then bust in and take her as easy as lifting a jug. Maybe get another key from the desk clerk. With a gun in her back, she wouldn't have raised any fuss. He noticed that she hadn't even turned her head when they'd hustled her down the front steps and into the stage.

Crazy assholes! The four of them ought to be playing with a string of spools. To snatch somebody half the damn country was already looking for! Stupid bastards were as good as wolf meat. God help them if they hurt her. He sighed. Anything they did, beginning with grabbing her, reflected on him; for everything, he was indirectly responsible. He could only hope she didn't start getting horny again. What was he saying? How could she *get* horny? With her it was a permanent condition.

They continued to avoid the built-up areas. Two shacks within a hundred yards of one another was enough to send them off the road and back on a half mile past. He was tempted to circle them wide at a gallop, get well ahead, stop in a town, send his wire to Doc, then get out of sight and wait for them to catch up. But he hesitated to chance it; if he ever lost them, his last chance to straighten out the whole mare's nest, slim as it was, would go down the well. Besides, where would he find a Western Union office open at this hour?

By the Big Dipper circling the North Star it was almost three in the morning when, after a stretch of close to eight miles without seeing so much as a single abandoned lean-to, they deserted the road. They made for a darkened sod house about two hundred yards distant, nestled in a group of hills. The soddy looked as if it had been vacant for ages: The roof was covered with weeds and wildflowers. The windows and door frame were nailed together from old packing cases. In place of window glass, oiled paper had been fixed to the frames. The gable roof, descending from its ridgepole, showed shakes along one edge.

This was not sod house country, he thought, pulling up alongside the road and watching them. It was much too far east. Central and western Nebraska, like Kansas, were dotted with soddies, but nobody built such a house in these parts. Yet there it stood. With all that growth on the roof and roots opening up the sod in a hundred places, in a heavy rain it no doubt leaked like a sieve. He had never understood why anybody would elect to live in a sod house, but then it was practically a last resort for homesteaders in places where timber was scarce. In such areas it was sod or canvas or the big blue roof. A soddy could be dangerous. When the roof soaked up enough water it got so heavy it could crack the ridgepole and cave in, burying the whole family under sod and muck. Even if the ridgepole held, bugs and mice, dirt and pebbles, were forever dropping from the ceiling into the soup or the baby's cradle.

Still, a soddy was better than a tent or a cave. It was cool in the summer and easy to keep warm in winter. It was fireproof, too; and with walls thirty inches thick, even a howling blizzard couldn't knock it over.

The merits and shortcomings of sod house living weren't exactly the first order of business at the moment, however. He dismounted, unfastened the reins, and hobbled the horse. It began nibbling grass contentedly. A good animal, he mused, patting its neck appreciatively, tough and agreeable. Few horses took such hard riding on such short notice from a stranger.

A line of saplings, a future wind- and snow-break, had been planted about fifty feet this side of the house. The driver had whipped his horses through an opening in the trees and come to a stop behind the house. Raider found the biggest hill in the group surrounding the house and flattened himself behind a convenient rock near the top of it to survey the scene. He couldn't see or even hear them going in the back door, but presently light showed around the edges of the oiled paper window within his view.

Four against one, with the Queen of Sheba in the middle. How could he possibly make a move? He lay prone, reflecting on this. A darkened figure stepped out the front door.

"Hey thar, Buster-Bob, the woman's okay, not a purty hair outta place, so y'all don't go tryin' nothin' rash, y'hear? G'night now."

A single shot rang out, passing him by a wide margin to the left and high overhead. He ducked instinctively.

Bastards! Getting up, he moved right, edging around to the rear of the house. The stage stood empty and eerie-looking in the silver-blue starlight. The horses had been unhitched and hobbled to feed. If he could get to them, free them . . . The bunch inside wouldn't get a hundred yards without horses. They wouldn't try. The nearest town out here had to be six miles distant in every direction. But loosing the horses would be like trying to bell a cat. One whinny, God forbid anything louder, and out the door the four would pile, throwing lead all over the landscape. Bad idea. A better one would be to catch some sleep, set his head for five o'clock, and wake up just before sunrise. Maybe pull something while they were still asleep. Ignoring the protesting sounds of his deprived stomach, he filled his hat with grass to make a pillow and went to sleep.

He was asleep a little more than an hour when the ground began to shake. He snapped awake. Indians! At least a hundred, galloping pell-mell down from the north, screaming like stricken banshees, wielding torches and lances, ancient rifles, and even cavalry swords, quickly surrounded the house. Light still lined the window frames. A dozen Indians dismounted and were looking over the stage. Others brought up the kidnappers' horses. Abruptly, like the lid popping off a stove, all hell broke loose, gunfire pouring forth from all four sides of the house.

"I don't believe those assholes! I purely don't!"

The Indians closest to the house began running in all directions. The others, farther removed, began fighting back. Fire arrows laced the darkness. One hit window paper, and it flared up briefly. The lamps inside went out.

Outnumbered twenty-five to one though they were, the defenders appeared to be quickly reducing the odds, but they were making a bad mistake, decided Raider; they were inviting destruction. Maybe they figured they were doomed regardless. Or maybe they had panicked. A dozen dead and badly wounded braves littered the ground, but the others were now hard at work, pouring everything they had at the house. The weeds on the roof caught fire; they would burn out without harming anything. The soddy was like a fort; the only way anybody outside could hit anybody inside was if the insider got careless. Not even a four-pounder could penetrate thirty inches of sod.

And yet, knowing the Indian mind as he did, Raider was sure that sooner or later they would rush the place, sacrificing two braves in order to get one inside with tomahawk in hand and blood in his eye.

Out of the night they had come to attack the house. The rods of light around the windows had announced it was occupied. Still, why this particular place? And why such a large war party? What were they? Not Pawnee—no red paint on their bodies or arrow headdresses; and not Omahas, who generally didn't attack anything on two legs. These looked to be Sioux, likely Oglalas. What, he wondered, were Crazy Horse's people doing this far east? They must be Oglalas; no mistaking the buffalo headdresses worn by the leaders, the quill chokers and bibs, the braids tightly bound in otter and even panther fur. Most of the warriors were bare to breech-clout or leggings, some with shells or silver disks fastened to their scalp locks and beads or a little mirror hanging on their chests. A rough bunch, he reflected; they could ride with the Comanches and shoot with any of their red kin. And took to white-eyes' arms like all the other Sioux.

The stink of gunpowder rose on the arriving breeze; the attackers were pouring everything they had at the soddy. Why? he asked himself for the sixth time. Why had they come? Just to steal horses? Not a bit. They wanted blood. They knew and wanted the four inside and appeared willing to lose a few of their own to get them. Suddenly a lone brave astride a little grulla came pounding down a hill, side-riding, seemingly bent on ramming the front door. But within six yards of it his pony shied; he lost his hold and tumbled to the ground. Up he sprang instantly, swinging his tomahawk, attacking the door, from which a lance and a dozen arrows already protruded. But all his fury, all his strength could not splinter the door. It was a gallant and totally useless effort, reflected Raider, watching. Then, unbelievably, the door was opened from the inside. For a long moment it stayed open; the brave dropped to the ground clutching his chest, shot dead. A hail of fire arrows poured inside. The door slammed. But brief though it was, the incident caused more than the death of the brave at the door; it also distracted the defenders within just long enough to permit five warriors to rush the burnt-out window and hurl their torches inside.

Two men came flying out the back door, firing with both hands—and were cut down before they got ten steps. As the taller of the two was hit full in the heart by an arrow and his knees started to buckle, a brave galloped by wielding a saber and lopped his head off. Blood spurted from the stump. A second brave deftly speared the head tumbling to rest a few feet away and held it up in triumph.

The shooting from inside the house stopped abruptly. The two surviving kidnappers emerged with their hands high. Quickly they were surrounded by braves on foot. Two of the leaders rode up and dismounted.

Why had they given up? wondered Raider. Had they run out of ammunition? Probably. They must know why they were being attacked, and knew as well that to surrender would gain them nothing, least of all their lives. Roped around the neck, their hands tied behind them, they were led away into the darkness.

Milena! Jesus Christ! In all the excitement he'd forgotten about her. She was dead; she had to be. The third and fourth ones coming out would have used her as a shield if she were still alive. He gulped, swallowed hard, and squinted, unable to believe his eyes. She was standing in the doorway.

"Don't do it. Don't kill her, you red fucks," he muttered.

They wouldn't. In a raid they might kill women, even children, but not a lone, unarmed, completely helpless survivor. He got to his knees, his hand on his Peacemaker. In minutes now they'd be clearing out, heading back to where they'd come from. And taking her with them. Which would be the last he'd ever see of her.

He was certain of it. He was wrong. It was not to be. Not this day, at any rate. Something pricked the back of his neck. What felt suspiciously like a muzzle thumped against his spine. He raised his hands as he got to his feet and turned slowly. There were three of them, grim-faced, menacing-looking, armed to their toothless mouths, packing everything but Gatling guns.

"Mornin', boys," said Raider.

CHAPTER SIX

Allan Pinkerton went away to Washington to confer with and placate President Grant, Secretary of War Belknap, and everybody else in positions of prominence with the federal government who had nothing better to do with their time than concern themselves with the disappearance of Queen and Pinkerton. At the chief's insistence, Doc Weatherbee would henceforth be working "hond in gloove" with Gillespie and Harrigan. King Nicholas insisted on sitting in on their meetings. He had no more interest in his queen's whereabouts or what she was up to than he'd had the day she vanished. Rather, as far as Doc could see, it was the excitement generated by her and Raider's disappearance and curiosity as to how the "experts" would go about recovering them that appealed to His Majesty.

Matters had reached a pass where Doc was convinced that the wrong queen had been kidnapped. Ernestine's affection for him was growing daily. It was, to say the least, a one-sided *affaire de coeur*. She was everywhere; she was triplets; every time he turned a corner, there she was. Hers was the first face he saw upon awakening and upon falling asleep.

The three Americans and the ruler of Montenegro sat in Gillespie's and Harrigan's room sifting through newspapers. By now, after four full days, Queen Milena's likeness had appeared in practically every newspaper in North America. Apart from promising all the reverberations of an international incident and encouraging the most outrageous rumors imaginable, the situation was become a breeding ground for innuendo. Every Pinkerton operative from San Francisco to Philadelphia had become the butt of tasteless comment, the wiseacres' prime target. Still to come were the reactions of foreign newspapers, not to mention heads of state. Sacks crammed to bursting with sympathetic mail addressed to King Nicholas had begun arriving. Queen Ernestine, too, was the target of nosy well-wishers. Mother and son were approached by not one but three well-known authors offering to write their respective life stories. The newspapers hadn't had it so bountiful and exciting since Boss Tweed was caught with New York City in his pocket.

Queen Ernestine took the hullabaloo in admirable stride. Doc had previously decided that she held little affection for her beautiful daughter-in-law. One might even say that she despised her and was ecstatic at her departure, delighting in the fact that it was under a cloud.

Ernestine's campaign to destroy Doc with love, coupled with Raider's dilemma and his own helplessness, were rapidly pushing the dapper one to the edge. He had taken to chain-smoking his favorite cheroots. Gillespie favored large green cigars. Between them they managed to keep the upper half of the room filled with smoke. The king did not complain; he was still much too disturbed by the cancellation of his buffalo hunt to care about anything as trifling as too much smoke in a room. Harrigan, however, was less tolerant.

"Either we open the doggone windows in this doggone hole or you two get rid of those stinking weeds, once and for all!"

Without a word, Gillespie got up and opened both windows. The smoke never budged.

"We've gotten sixteen telegrams the past two days," said Gillespie, "placing the two of them in sixteen different towns from Wichita Falls, Texas, to Dickinson, North Dakota, and as far east as Bayonne, New Jersey." He laughed raucously. "They're covering more territory than a two-wagon road show."

"What's so funny?" asked Doc.

"Aw come on, don't be so serious. They've got to be someplace. We'll catch up with them. Somebody will."

"Every one o' those leads turned out phony," interposed Harrigan. "You boys want to know what I think?"

Doc and Gillespie said no with their expressions. Nicholas spoke.

"Yes, yes."

"I think they're holed up right here in Kansas City, right under our noses."

Gillespie scoffed. "That's dumb."

"Is it? You ever read *The Purloined Letter,* by Edgar Allan Poe? The police looked all over creation for a blackmail letter, and all the time it was right there in the blackmailer's house."

Doc had had about all he could take from both Gillespie and Harrigan. They were about as much help in solving the thing as oars on a prairie schooner, one of Raider's pet observations. How much longer he could go on working "hond in gloove," as he'd been instructed, remained to be seen; but he wouldn't bet on more than an hour, the way things were proceeding. Gillespie was proving himself the prince of pompous asses, blessed with all the brains and common sense of a gatepost. Harrigan wasn't nearly as bright, in addition to which all he did was complain: about the food, the weather, the dearth of leads, his bunions, Gillespie's cigars . . .

Poor Rade, he thought, where could he have gotten to? What the devil was going on? He had to be in some kind of bind or Doc would have heard from him by now. Was he hurt? Was he dead? Sixteen wires claimed the two of them had been seen in sixteen different locales. With her picture all over the continent, in practically every newspaper, on every lawman's wall, on handbills and posters, with the offer of a $25,000 reward, it was inconceivable that no leads had turned up.

They could, of course, be holed up on a farm, along with whoever had helped her plan the thing. A farm, a mining camp, any out-of-the-way place. They could be on a train heading down to El Paso and over the border into Mexico.

She obviously wanted to hide out, which might explain their failure to come up with any leads. On the other hand, it was possible they'd run into trouble. Raider could handle anything, even Indians. But having her along, and who could say how many others, could complicate matters.

Rade was all he cared about, not her, certainly not her accomplices, not the agency, not big-mouth "Unconditional Surrender." The plowboy only. If her shenanigans got him hurt or worse, there would be hell to pay!

"And I'll be the collection agent."

"What are you talking about?" asked Gillespie.

Doc got up, stumped out his cheroot, and stretched. "Nothing, just thinking out loud."

"Where are you going?" Harrigan asked.

"Out. I need fresh air. I want to think."

"Think about Kansas City, *The Purloined Letter*. We should conduct a sweep of this burg. From the west side all the way to the docks. It wouldn't hurt, would it, Gil?"

"Sure wouldn't. We've got to start somewheres."

That's good, thought Doc. Here we are, coming up on day five, and we've got to start somewhere. Lovely. It's a pleasure working with you boys.

Reaching the lobby, he was starting out the door when a voice called to him. It was the desk clerk, a middle-aged woman with hair like wire, parted in the middle and twisted in tight little spirals around her ears. She was discouragingly plain-looking, with a strange nose—oversized, aquiline, starting out from the usual site and veering slightly to the left. She stared at him, hand upraised, and made a halfhearted effort to smile.

"Dr. Weatherlee?"

"Weatherbee."

He retraced his steps.

"A telegram came for Mr. Pinkerton. He's checked out. You and he . . ."

"I'll take it."

"Sure, though you'll have to sign for it, being as you're not the addressee."

He signed, tore open the envelope, and read the message. His jaw dropped slowly, his face exploding in a grin. Making a fist, he hammered the air and whooped loudly.

CHAPTER SEVEN

"This has been the most exciting experience of my entire life!" exclaimed Milena.

Raider covered his face with his hands and dug the tips of his fingers into his eyes. "Exciting," he repeated flatly, his palms muffling his voice. Down came his hands. "I keep tellin' myself you're crazy, you know that? But that's just, you know, an expression. Only now I think you really got to be nuttier than a damn jaybird with his skull cracked! Have you got the faintest idea what we're gettin' into? What you got us into?"

"We're going to visit Indians."

"Visit . . ."

He stared out the window of the stage at the graying sky; the sun was coming up. He was tired, hungry, his jewels still hurt, and he was worried sick. Where they were heading, how long it would take them to get there didn't concern him in the slightest. What would happen once they arrived did, mightily. If all the tribes had one thing in common it was their treatment of white captives. The squaws beat the living hell out of the women; the young bucks beat the living hell out of the men. Skinning alive was a favorite pastime— ventilating a man's hide just to see the pretty blood spurt out, poking as many holes as they could before his lamp doused. They could also hamstring him—draw cords through slits cut at his heel tendons and make him march around the camp until he collapsed. The worst thing they could do would be to turn him over to the women and children; they'd put on a real gala for the warriors and wind up tearing the top of his scalp off and pouring red-hot coals over his pretty brain.

The best he could hope for would be that they'd cut his hair off and set him to pounding corn or cutting up buffalo meat with the women. To give the men something to poke fun at.

Milena was lucky they weren't Yavapais. If they were she could end up tattooed like Olive Oatman. He'd heard stories of another woman, Fanny Kelly, who'd been kidnapped by the Oglalas. They'd beaten and starved her, but she'd gotten off easy compared with other captive white women. Most got themselves raped by half the tribe and wound up tied to an unbroken pony which was whipped to a gallop, running up and down a gauntlet, while braves shot arrows into the burden on its back. Yea, brother, considering the white man's experience under the red man's thumb, life promised to be as harsh as hell with the heat up, he reflected gloomily, particularly for one used to good living and all the regal comforts. And wait till they got around to passing her from tepee to tepee. If she got out of that round robin alive she'd likely never look a cock in the eye again. And if she tried to get away and they caught her, which they would, she could say good-bye to the top of her head. Exciting, shit!

"What are you thinking about?" she asked brightly.

She looked as if she'd had ten hours' sleep: Her eyes were clear, every hair was in place, her patronizing smile was intact, and there wasn't a single wrinkle in her dress.

"Did those mangy bastards back in the soddy, ah . . . do . . ."

"Did they attack me? Oh, no. Once, the leader did make an obscene remark, but I chastized him on the spot. He hardly opened his mouth after that. To me, at any rate."

"How much did they fix on askin' for you?"

"Fifty thousand dollars. Can you imagine? The silly creatures. I am of royal blood, the ruler of a country, revered by my subjects, and considered the most beautiful queen in the history of Montenegro. A piddling fifty thousand! I've

never been so insulted! But, of course, I've never been to
America before.''

"Along 'bout now you must be wishin' you never set foot
on the damn boat.''

"Must you swear every other word?''

He grunted and swore under his breath. They trundled
along in silence. The musty odor of the stage was making him
sick to his empty stomach. They were surrounded by their
captors. They seemed to be heading west. They had crossed
the Big Blue River and would cross it again where it curved
southward, passing on the near side of Marquette. They
would probably travel all day. A happy prospect. He was
already so famished his stomach felt as if it had shrunk to
approximately the size of a baseball.

"They feed you?'' he asked.

"Yes, worse luck. Some absolutely disgusting beans and a
bread of some kind that tasted like sawdust. And coffee, if
you can call it that. It was vile.''

"No roast pheasant or fifty-buck wine? No little chocolates
with nuts stuck on top?''

"Aren't we amusing, though.''

"Hey, you know somethin'? It's 'bout time you came
down from your high horse. You got us into this pickle,
which the chances are better than good neither one of us is
gonna get out of alive. The least you can do is start treatin'
me a little better than whoever you got shovels out your damn
stable. You may not like the idea, lady, but you need me.''

She stared at him. A smile softened her face, bringing a
sparkle to her eyes. She edged closer to him, slipping her arm
through his.

"I do indeed.''

"It's only fair to warn you, it's not gonna be any high old
party, with fiddles an' sugar cakes, when we get there. It
could easy turn out rough as a cob.''

"Nonsense. They have no cause to mistreat us.''

"The last thing Indians need is a reason. They make folks
bleed for the pure fun of it.''

"You're forgetting one thing: I'm a queen.''

"Make sure you tell 'em when we get there. It'll make a big difference."

"Stop fretting. Everything will be just fine."

"Sure, an' after we've stayed our welcome an' you start feelin' bored, what are you gonna do, ask old Crazy Horse to send out for a couple o' train tickets back to Kansas City?"

"Is that where Nicky and Mother Monster are?" She tittered icily. "No, thank you, that's the last place we'll be going."

"Then count me out."

"Now, don't be angry. And don't pout; you look like a little boy. I know what you need."

Her hand slipped across his thigh and began unbuttoning his fly.

"Lay off, will you? We're in deep sh . . . We're in the fix to end all fixes. How can you even think 'bout foolin' round, for chrissakes?"

He sputtered irritably, fuming and fussing; but, curiously, he made no move to remove or escape her warm and prying fingers.

The sun was setting when they arrived at the Oglalas' camp. It was typical—a hundred-odd tepees, smoldering fires, dogs attacking bones and running around, naked children, squaws squatting in groups, chattering, gossiping. Loud laughter and horseplay. Two ancient squaws seemed to be the only ones working, down on their knees slicing away at antelope carcasses. Another squaw was heaping green branches on a cook fire to raise smoke to drive away the mosquitoes, gnats, and green flies. The returning braves were greeted with loud cheers. The entire tribe assembled around the stage coach; they peered in the windows, poked at the sides, and a couple of youngsters even crawled underneath to examine it. The Oglalas had brought back their dead, about twenty corpses slung across ponies. Squaws recognizing their men ran to them screaming hysterically, throwing themselves against the bodies. Milena started.

"That bunch is our welcomin' committee."

"I do not understand."

Raider restored his manhood to its habitat and buttoned his fly.

"You're lookin' at brand-new widows, lady. When they spot the color o' our skins they're gonna' be a little bit upset. They got to know their brothers and their daddies didn't kill their husbands."

"I did not shoot a single bullet. I wanted to, but Hamer would not give me a gun. I am an excellent shot, you know. I hunt. I also practice shooting at targets."

"Good for you. By the way, did this Hamer or any of his friends ever mention why the Indians were gunnin' for them?"

"No"

"They musta had a beef o' some sort."

The door was opened; they got out. The chief emerged from his tepee. His appearance drew all eyes. He was not the typical overly ornamented and painted Sioux warrior. His skin was unusually pale for an Indian's. He wore no paint, no feathers. His hair, braided tightly and wrapped in panther fur, looked soft and was much lighter than any Indian's Raider had ever seen before; it was almost blond. When Crazy Horse was twenty-six he had stolen Black Buffalo Woman from her husband, No Water, for which No Water had shot him in the face. The scar disfigured his entire right cheek and part of his nose, and to add to his humiliation Black Buffalo Woman deserted him. He then took an Oglala, Black Shawl, as his squaw.

He was one of the greatest of the fighting Oglalas—respected, held in awe even by the whites taking over his lands and by his blood enemies, the Snakes and Crows. He was actually a Brulé with Oglala blood and a little Minneconjou, even a little Cheyenne, and on both sides Lakota.

His history to date was one of violence and bloodshed. He was twelve when he killed his first enemy, an Omaha squaw. Four years later his childhood name of Curly was changed to Crazy Horse, his father's, a tribal holy man's name. He fought with the warriors against the Snakes. From then on he fought so many battles with other tribes and the white trespassers that even he could not keep count of all the times, the places, the wounds.

Beside him, wearing so many shells, coins, claws, beads, and feathers and painted so many colors he resembled a Christmas tree, stood He-Dog, his brother-friend. Raider had never met Crazy Horse, but had seen He-Dog's picture, and recognized him immediately.

Crazy Horse's people formed a pathway from where he and He-Dog were standing to the two white captives. Two braves grabbed Raider and Milena and pushed them forward.

They stood before the chief. He ran his fingers down Milena's face. She glared and started to protest. Raider grabbed her arm and squeezed it hard.

"You're hurting me!" she hissed.

"Don't make him mad, for chrissakes, he's the damn host."

This advice, sage and timely though it may have been, cost the adviser dearly. A war club slammed him in the shoulder, tumbling him in a heap. His shoulder was broken in ten places, or so it felt. He got up slowly, dusting himself off, his teeth clenched, fighting back the pain.

"Are you all right?" she asked.

He said nothing. The fee for talking was, he decided, exorbitant.

Doc reread the telegram. It was like an eight-pound gold nugget dropped in his lap. Nothing was happening in the case, not the faintest glimmer of a lead, not even a halfway credible rumor that might be worth their decamping Kansas City.

Now this. It was from a Marshal Ephraim Tucker up in Pawnee City, just above the border. The marshal had two prisoners—"foreigners." He had arrested them, charging them with destruction of property, specifically, most of the lobby of the Pawnee House. A second charge was attempted murder of one Oscar Schofield, the desk clerk. All of which would ordinarily have held scant interest for Doc. It was Tucker's last two lines that aroused that interest:

BELIEVE THEM TO BE FROM MONTENEGRO STOP APPEAR TO
RECOGNIZE NEWSPAPER PICTURE OF MISSING QUEEN

He stood by his bed hurling his belongings into his battered alligator rubber gladstone bag. He would have to buy a horse and saddlebags; a rifle might come in handy. If he were to end up down behind a rock, his Diamondback empty in his fist, it certainly would. How far was Pawnee City, he wondered? He got out his map of the Plains states and measured it off using his four-inch I.D. card for a ruler. He estimated it to be about ninety miles—allowing for bends in the road. He groaned aloud. Riding a horse ten miles was uncomfortable for one accustomed to an upholstered wagon seat; ninety miles in the saddle promised pure torture. Still, dwelling on the unavoidable only made it worse. Snapping shut the bag, he took a quick look around the dingy little room and left. Down in the lobby, surrendering his key and paying his bill, he suddenly remembered Gillespie and Harrigan.

Remembered them and promptly forgot them.

"He travels fastest who travels without Gillespie and Harrigan."

Less than an hour later Kansas City was behind him. Heading northwest, he crossed the Missouri border and would recross it to reach Leavenworth. He planned to ride all night. By the time he reached Pawnee City the horse, a barrel-chested bay stallion, would be on the brink of collapse, as would he himself. Small sacrifice indeed, and he welcomed the discomfort destined for his derriere if it meant finding Raider even as little as one hour sooner. Raider *and* Queen Milena, providing they were still together. They should be. He hoped they'd be!

He rested twice—at one in the morning and at a quarter to five. He had traveled at a reasonable pace, sparing the horse, mindful that the road ahead was much too long to blow it out before the halfway point. Into Pawnee City the stallion trotted at eight o'clock in the morning by Doc's ancient but most reliable Waterbury watch. Marshal Tucker's office was not hard to find, not with the four-foot sign announcing MARSHAL above the door.

Tucker was sitting at his open curtain-top desk in a dilapidated chair, leafing through a stack of wanted dodgers. He was a gray man, gray with years—hair, eyes, mustache, teeth, shirt. Letting fly a strool of tobacco juice, skillfully bull's-eyeing the spittoon in the corner, he swung back around and examined his visitor up and down. Doc held up his I.D. card.

"Morning, Marshal, Doc Weatherbee's the name. Pinkertons. You sent a telegram to Allan Pinkerton. He left Kansas City for Washington to meet with President Grant, so I took the liberty of signing for it."

"Have a chair, Dr. Weatherbee."

Doc sat, winced, and stifled a groan. He tried one cheek; he tried the other. The pain was impartial.

"I take it you been riding all night. Mister, you need a hosing down and ten hours' sleep. I bet you could eat boiled wolf."

"Right on all counts. Are you still holding the two Montenegrins?"

Tucker nodded, shifted his chaw from one cheek to the other, and grinned.

"Till Judge Gaitenbee comes to town. They done close to a thousand bucks' damage over to the Pawnee House. Nearly killed Oscar Schofield, the desk clerk. Would have if Mrs. Purly hadn't come a-running. It took seven of us to get the two of 'em down and hog-tied. Like I said in the telegram, neither one speaks English, nary a word. Some foreign lingo. Sounds like Injun to me."

"It's almost identical to Serbo-Croatian."

"Do tell."

"How did you know they were Montenegrins?"

"When we searched 'em we found papers with the royal seal on 'em. Like the one they printed in the newspaper with the picture o' the queen."

"Go on."

"Both were mad as hornets at Oscar."

"What did he do to them?"

Tucker scratched his head. "Nothing, so he claims. Doesn't know why they come after him, and neither o' them give a reason, not in any words I'd savvy."

"You said in your telegram that they appeared to recognize Queen Milena from her picture in the paper."

He held up a copy of the Pawnee City *Gazette and Courier*, showing the queen's picture, crown, ermine, royal seal, and all.

"They were staying at the hotel and she was too, is that it?"

"They sure were, but if she was, nobody told me." Again he scratched his head. "To tell the truth, I never did think to ask. It didn't seem important at the time, what with all the ruckus. But when we subdued 'em and brought 'em in to lock up, the biggest one spotted this and recognized her. And started kicking up another fuss, jabbering away, getting all red in the face again. Another thing, he had a bump on his head the size of a hen's egg. I spotted it, and I recollect thinking at the time that getting hit over the head to raise a bump like that could make a man a little short o' hat size, if you follow my meaning. Seems like she had to be staying there if they were."

"Schofield would know." Doc got up wearily, stretched, and pulled his sweaty trousers free of his aching cheeks.

"Want to see those two out back?"

"Yes, but first Schofield. Do you know where I can find him?"

"It's too early for him to be at work. He's got a room at the Pawnee House, but at the moment he's likely feeding his face at Utterby's." He gestured. "Down the street, turn right, second door. Utterby's; name's on both windows."

"What does he look like?"

"About your age, straight blond hair that kinda slants down his forehead off to one side. Light blue eyes. Wears specs sometimes, silver-rim jobs. Skinny as a rake. Nice young fellow; the missus is always saying she wonders why he hasn't got himself hitched. Works steady, studying something or other mail order on the side, regular churchgoer, honest as Abe.''

"I'll find him." He shook Tucker's hand. "Thanks for your time, Marshal, and thanks a load for taking the trouble to wire us. We were getting nowhere. You know there's a reward—"

"I know, the missus keeps telling me, and I keep telling her peace officers aren't supposed to accept rewards, not in Nebraska they aren't. We get paid for what we do, though not much." He snickered. "Still, nobody twisted my arm so's they could get this badge on me. See you later.''

He let fly another brown missile. His aim was remarkable, mused Doc as he left. He never missed the hole. The drip plate it centered was shining clean.

Oscar Schofield was finishing his breakfast, a red and white checkered napkin tucked in his collar and decorated with two worm-size spatterings of egg yolk. Utterby's was mobbed, patrons jammed in back to back around some twenty tables in a space that could comfortably accommodate no more than a dozen. The two waitresses squeezed their way about. Doc introduced himself to Schofield, taking the chair opposite him. He quickly covered all the ground covered in Tucker's office, then started on new territory. He produced a reward poster displaying Queen Milena's picture, unfolded it carefully, and held it up for Schofield's appraisal.

"She was registered at the Pawnee House, right?"

Doc had been a Pinkerton a little more than a year, but into that brief time he had crammed considerable experience in dealing with all types representing the well-known walks of life. He found he had something of a gift for recognizing lies and evasions. In response to his question Schofield did not lie. He did not evade. What he did was hesitate. His gaze wandered slightly to the left of Doc's sight line, breaking the contact between their eyes, and his tongue moistened his lips nervously. Both these signs gave him away. Realizing it, he tried to expunge Doc's suspicion before it could root.

"Yes," he snapped.

"And the two who attacked you were guarding her."

"Yes."

"She checked out, and when they found out they went after you. Look, instead of my asking sixty-three questions, why don't you tell me exactly what happened?"

He had been on duty the day before yesterday early in the evening when three men walked in, demanding to see Queen Milena. He had told them that no such person was registered and showed them the book as proof. One of them pulled a gun and forced him to hand over the spare key to her room. They went up the stairs, came back down with her, and left.

"That was the last I saw of any of them."

"How come you didn't call the law?"

"How could I? The one with the gun stood there pointing it at me while the others went up after her."

"Was anybody else in the lobby?"

"Only Frank Pacelli, the barber. He was asleep under a newspaper, snoring to beat the band."

"So they left."

"I was going to alert the marshal the second they walked out, but I never got the chance. One of the big oafs with her was upstairs. He came running down, rubbing the back of his head. The other came running in from outside. They were furious, carrying on like madmen. Then they started tearing the place apart, and me with it."

"There was another man with the queen."

"There was?"

Schofield widened his eyes; they shifted upward in their sockets ever so slightly. The man was a poor liar. Doc paused a moment to mull over what he already had. He could go back to the marshal's office and work on the two Montenegrins, but why bother? Why waste precious time struggling through pantomime for bits and pieces of information? Clearly, Schofield had all the answers.

The clerk wiped his mouth with his napkin, sipped his coffee, and put on an expression of earnestness so exaggerated Doc nearly burst out laughing.

"Ahem, there's a $25,000 reward for her safe return."

"You continue to cooperate and you're in line for it, maybe first in line."

Schofield beamed.

"There's something else you're first in line for."

"What?"

"Twenty-five years in the state penitentiary at Lincoln." Doc got up, his face as grim as he could make it. "A pleasure talking to you, Mr. Schofield. Enjoy your breakfast. We'll be in touch."

"Wait a minute, wait a minute. What are you saying? What are you talking about, penitentiary? Mister, you've got a strange sense of humor."

"Aiding and abetting kidnapping is worth twenty-five years minimum. Of course if the whole scheme was yours to begin with, you could swing. And I can think of at least two people who'll do everything in their power to see that you do. Allan Pinkerton and Ulysses S. Grant." He leaned over the table and lowered his voice. "I'm leaving. I'll wait outside one minute. One. I want to give you every chance to square yourself, but I haven't got all day. You want to talk privately, I'm agreeable. If you don't want to talk at all, if you prefer to go on spinning tall tales, you can tell them to a judge and jury. Oscar, I'm not interested. Good day."

He walked out. Standing outside, he counted eight seconds before Schofield appeared. Doc nodded across the street.

"That alley looks nice and private."

Schofield's self-confidence had completely deserted him. His pale cheeks were flushed, he stuttered slightly getting his words out, he flung his hands about and shifted his weight from one leg to the other, back and forth. Yes, Raider had also arrived with the queen, but he'd gone out with the shorter of the two Montenegrins and never come back. The four men who had kidnapped her were the Iverson brothers, Hamer, Luke, Ira, and Orland. Yes, he'd told them she'd come to Pawnee City and was registered at the hotel, but abducting her was their idea, not his. This he insisted on repeatedly; this, in particular, Doc didn't believe a word of.

"Where did they take her?"

"I swear to God in heaven I don't know."

"Oscar . . ."

"All right, all right, but I'm cooperating, right? I'm painting the whole picture for you. I should be entitled to the reward. I should."

Doc stared aghast. He lit a cheroot. The man was a marvel. He practically had the rope around his neck with the trap bolt sliding loose under his feet and here he was talking reward.

"Oscar, you are one of a kind. Answer the question."

"They've got a place up the line, a sod house. I think a cousin or uncle of theirs built it. It's been vacant some time."

"Where up the line?"

"No town, not for miles. I guess the closest to it is Eagle, on the far side."

"You guess . . ."

Schofield gestured helplessly. "I've never seen the place. I hardly know the Iversons."

"You know them enough to do business with them. Let's go."

"Where?"

"To jail, where do you think?"

Doc took hold of his arm. Schofield shook it off. Annoyance quickly supplanted his fear.

"You can't. How come? I'm cooperating. You haven't asked a single question I haven't answered. It's almost eight-thirty. I've got to get to work."

"You're going to jail, Oscar, for complicity in kidnapping. The Iversons never would have known she was under your roof if you didn't tell them. Let's cut the nonsense, shall—"

He stopped short. Anger flooded Schofield's eyes. He scowled and swung. Doc ducked, bringing up his right hand, and caught him full in the stomach, doubling him over. Groaning pathetically, he held the position until grabbed by the shirtfront and straightened.

"Don't do that again. Move."

•   •   •

Raider and one of the Montenegrins had been out when the Iversons left with the queen. Probably together. Unquestionably. Raider would have to be watched every moment he was out of her sight. Maybe the two of them came back just in time to see the kidnappers leaving town and spotted her with them. Raider hadn't gone back inside. He certainly hadn't just wandered off. No, he had chased them. His companion had not, probably because he was worried about his partner, suspecting that he had tried to stop the abduction and paid for it. Had Raider caught up with them, he wondered, or was he still pursuing?

He turned a now surprisingly subdued Schofield over to Marshal Tucker, who locked him up even before hearing Doc's explanation. After he did, he let Doc into the Montenegrins' cell. An uneasy feeling crept through his mind as Tucker relocked the door. Either of them could break him in half with his bare hands. Happily, all the fight appeared to have gone out of them. Doc showed them the poster with Queen Milena's picture.

"Must find her. Must . . ."

He felt like an imbecile talking so. They stared blankly. He showed his I.D. card.

"Detective. Police. *Polizei*."

He couldn't tell whether they understood or were simply impressed by the official-looking card in his hand, but both suddenly looked relieved, and the shorter one even went so far as to pat him on the shoulder. However, eliciting any additional information looked to be impossible. Doc was not skilled in exotic languages, and they, apparently, didn't know two words of English. But they weren't stupid. The shorter one pantomimed a request for paper and pencil. Could he write English? wondered Doc. He called out to Tucker and the marshal brought a pencil and a small yellow pad. The man sat on his cot and drew the rough outline of a stagecoach. Doc nodded. Holding the sketch in one hand, he described himself as Raider with the other, taller, broader, stronger, wearing a mustache, gun, and holster. He then pantomimed Raider chasing the stage. The man nodded vigorously.

Doc kept at it patiently, confirming that the man had seen Raider run around the corner, then had gone back inside. Common sense suggested that Raider would never have caught them on foot, but once around the corner could probably have stolen a horse. One good thing: He had his gun with him.

Neither had much more to add. Doc thanked them profusely and called to Tucker, who came and let him out. They went and stood outside the front door.

"What's your next move?" the marshal asked.

"Get something to eat and catch a couple hours' sleep."

"You'll need more than that."

"I can't afford more."

"I could alert the whole area up by Eagle, even ring in the Army from headquarters in Omaha."

"Maybe, but not right away. Kidnapping's a ticklish business. Sometimes one or two can accomplish a lot more than big numbers. The first consideration is her safety, obviously."

"True, but by your lonesome you may not even find the place."

"There can't be too many sod houses up there. About those Montenegrins: Everything I've been able to dig up since I got here is making them look better and better. You have to agree, there were extenuating circumstances."

"I reckon. Still, the damage was done. Who should pay for it if they don't?"

"How about Schofield? None of this would have happened if he hadn't gotten his bright idea. For a fine, upstanding, hardworking churchgoer he's a bit greedy, wouldn't you say? I get the impression he started cooking up this mess all of sixty seconds after he found out who she was." He paused. "How did he, I wonder? It's possible my partner inadvertently tipped him off. Maybe Oscar spotted the royal crests on her luggage. Can you recommend a rooming house?"

"First you eat, then you sleep. I'm taking you home, friend."

Tucker locked the door and they started out. They didn't get more than ten steps before a man came running up the street waving both hands, calling loudly to the marshal. Tucker sighed.

"Cletus Arthur Toombs, the mortician. Somebody stole his horse day before yesterday and he's been pestering the hell out of me to get it back. I keep telling him it's long gone, but he won't listen."

CHAPTER EIGHT

The tepee stunk: human sweat, rotten meat, and feces. In the center was a fire circle. To the right of it was a painted bull buffalo skull, a sacred totem of the animal and the herds and good hunting luck to the owner of the lodge: He-Dog.

Raider rested on his shins, his arms behind him. His wrists were tied tightly to his ankles, so tightly it felt like hot wires clamped around all four joints. He was naked, his body blackened with ashes all over, and his hair had been hacked off with a tomahawk. But not his scalp. For the moment it was intact, as was the rest of his blackened body. But the pain of his bindings was becoming more than he could stand. He was on the verge of passing out.

It was hot in the tepee, but he was shivering. Emerging sweat formed slender patches in the soot covering him. He had been fed: greasy jerky and something he couldn't identify that tasted like raw kidney. And he had been forced to down a gourd of blood, which he promptly vomited, incurring the wrath of He-Dog's two squaws. One had stripped off his clothes while the other held a knife at his nose. Then they tied him up and scrubbed his body with ashes. A freshly killed buffalo cow was brought up, and with other squaws the two had butchered it, cutting and slashing, laughing and arguing, snacking on raw liver, kidneys, the tongue, the eyes, belly fat, chewing gristle from the snout, marrow from the leg bones, and fighting over the tastiest morsels of all, the hoofs of an unborn calf. An old woman sliced the nipples and drank the warm milk. The belly was slit with great ceremony and the entrails removed, warriors joining the feast, kneeling and drinking handfuls of warm blood. No one touched the brains. They were a delicacy reserved for He-Dog, Raider knew.

He had not seen Milena since sundown the day before. Crazy Horse's squaw, Black Shawl, a small thin woman with sad eyes and a livid scar that looked like a rope burn cradling her throat, had led the queen away. Would he ever see her again? he wondered.

His shoulder, smashed by the war club, was intact but badly swollen, and it ached furiously. His mouth tasted foul. When he threw up the blood, the jerky and the raw kidney or liver, whatever it was, had come up with it, and now he was hungrier than ever.

He guessed it was about ten o'clock in the morning. After the butchering they had brought him inside, forcing him to kneel trussed up all night while He-Dog and his two squaws slept, enjoyed intercourse, argued, and finally went back to sleep. They had given him as much attention as they did the buffalo skull.

Again he wondered what had happened to Milena. Was she having the gay old time she planned on, and seriously? Had she gotten around to tasting buffalo blood? He shook his head and grunted. It was as close to the red wine on the menu on the train as she'd get in this Garden of Eden. Knowing her, though, she'd probably tasted blood and asked for seconds. It wouldn't surprise him; nothing about her, nothing she did would ever surprise him again. Still, she wouldn't put Crazy Horse in his place as easily as she put Pinkertons and every other male. The chief's squaw, Black Shawl, puny as she looked, wouldn't put up with it. A sick woman, Black Shawl, coughing constantly; the galloping consumption for sure.

The shaft of light slanting in through the opened flap cut off sharply. He lifted his eyes from the dead fire. There stood Milena in deerskins and moccasins, her hair in braids, a beaded band around her head, a single brown and white hawk feather poking up from the back. Minnehaha in the flesh, he thought, marveling. As usual, she looked as if she'd just stepped out of her beauty bath.

"Having a good time?" he asked in a surly tone.

"Merciful St. Basil, you look dreadful!" She tittered. "And ridiculous. What have they done to you?"

"What does it look like? Can you loosen my wrists? This rawhide's squeezing me to death. I'm about to pass out."

He did, falling to one side. She brought him back to consciousness moments later. He opened his eyes. She was slapping his face lightly between attempts to get water down him. It was warm but clean. She had untied him and brought a blanket, helping him wrap it around his waist to cover his nakedness. He began massaging the circulation back into his fingers and wrists and upper arms. Putting all his weight on his shins had nearly fractured his knee joints. He rubbed them gingerly.

"You do good work, Your Highness. Now you'd best get outta here before one of 'em catches you."

Too late. He-Dog showed at the flap. Raider had seen tough-looking Indians before, but He-Dog led the pack. His face was a mass of sharp angles and looked as if it had been sculptured in bronze, then held over a fire to blacken it. He was wearing a war bonnet with a four-foot row of eagle feathers down the back, each one decorated with bright stripes of beadwork at the base and tipped with a plume fashioned from the hair of a white horse. And each feather was cut, alternating notches for enemies slain and slices for throats slit. The bonnet made him look six feet tall; when he took it off to get through the opening he dropped a foot in height and with it much of his commanding appearance.

Still, he looked fiercer than most Raider had seen. His eyes and mouth were horizontal slits that appeared to be filed in his metallic face. Coming in, he pushed Milena out. Back in she came instantly, berating him for his bad manners.

Raider sighed to himself. Any second He-Dog would pull the knife at his belt and jam it into her hilt deep.

"Get out like he wants, Milena, for chrissakes!"

His unexpected outburst startled her, and she backed

toward the opening but refused to leave. Ignoring her, He-Dog squatted in front of Raider, glaring grimly and jabbering. Raider knew no Sioux, only a little Crow and a half-dozen words of Cheyenne. But he could hand-talk fairly well, and among the tribes reading hands was everybody's skill. He raised his palm in greeting. Then he drew his finger across his throat, denoting a Sioux, and placed his right hand on his left chest, moving it out to the right. "Sioux good." An obvious fawning compliment, but the effect was positive. He-Dog stopped talking and almost smiled. Raider went on to describe himself as the Oglalas' friend—not a soldier, not a liar, not a hunter of the buffalo, nobody who either posed a threat or competed with the "mighty Oglalas." Only a fool would take a man's word for his own character, he mused, as he continued talking, but if it accomplished nothing else it was at least getting blood back into his fingers.

He didn't convince He-Dog of his friendship and peaceful nature. He didn't raise his doubts. Raider evidently puzzled him. So much so that he got up and walked out. He came back a minute later with Crazy Horse. Milena stood aside, a display of deference that surprised Raider. She nodded to Crazy Horse, smiling.

"You are a friend to our people?" Crazy Horse asked Raider. "Or is it that you are afraid to die and lie to keep your scalp?"

"I have never harmed the Sioux. I have never harmed any Indian."

"Except in self-defense." Crazy Horse laughed without smiling. "The squaws want to kill you. You refused to drink blood."

"I didn't refuse, Chief. I drank it, I just couldn't keep it down. My stomach was empty."

"You will be fed, then you will drink blood. I myself will give it to you."

"If it's okay with you, give it to me now before I eat anything."

"Now." He turned to Milena.

She stared at Raider pityingly, then went out. She returned

minutes later carrying a turtle shell half filled with blood. Crazy Horse took it from her. He-Dog was grinning through his rotted teeth in earnest now, his slit eyes fastened on Raider. Crazy Horse handed him the shell.

"Drink."

He took a deep breath, steeled his gut, reminded himself of what could happen to him if he duplicated his previous performance, shot a last glance at the gleaming knife in He-Dog's belt, and drank.

It hit bottom. Instantly, nausea was tugging at his stomach like an attacking hand. His juices roiled protestingly. The sick feeling hurled itself upward, up his throat into his mouth. He belched loudly but did not retch, battling down the urge to, winning, holding the grisly, warm, and salty contents of his stomach.

Crazy Horse nodded approvingly to He-Dog, who scowled. Crazy Horse pushed Milena gently outside; he and He-Dog followed her. Raider was alone. Again he belched, and a third time. Nausea exploded in his stomach. Up came the blood, shooting from his throat like a projectile, arcing in front of him, splattering into the dead fire. Quickly he covered it with ashes, wiped his mouth, and spat in an effort to rid it of the disgusting taste. He cast about, looking for the gourd Milena had used for the water she'd given him. It was empty.

He had passed his first test. He'd cheated but had gotten away with it. The first, but not the last.

Two squaws brought him food—more dried jerky and a foul-smelling mush of some kind that had to be corn gone rotten. He tasted it but couldn't bring himself to eat any. The jerky he devoured. It conjured up visions of hoofs and horns, but the taste wasn't salty, which was a relief. He ate slowly, filling his stomach, appeasing his hunger. He could almost feel his strength coming back. He would need it, he thought gloomily. Crazy Horse was a cut above He-Dog, smarter, better able to control his temper, able to speak English, which was a help, but more fond of playing games with him than helping him.

Him? What about her?

He smiled a smile of admiration. She was apparently doing just fine. Dressing up like a squaw, handing her things over to Black Shawl before she pulled them off her was a wise move. The Queen of Monte . . . whatever it was. She had her faults, all the ones all pampered and spoiled women had, but she sure had a flair for adapting to circumstances. She hadn't had much success with He-Dog, but him she didn't need on her side. Crazy Horse was in charge, and they seemed to be getting along famously.

Was that good or bad? A little of each. Good because it kept her alive, and as long as she was around she'd protect him if she could. Bad because the more Crazy Horse liked her, the more she pretended to like him, the less chance he would let her go. Either of them. And Black Shawl in the middle wouldn't be any help.

No, he'd never let them walk. He had no reason to. Which meant they would have to escape. And successfully, or be dragged back by the ankles as dead as the buffalo he'd just eaten.

Crazy Horse would not let them walk. Escape was a thousand-to-one shot. Which left rescue.

"Figurin' all the angles, what are the odds on that?" he asked himself aloud. "Two thousan' to one? Three? Oh, Doc, wherever you are, whatever you're doin', drop it. Come, an' come fast!"

His hope was a vain one. By its nature, following his and Milena's trail could not possibly be accelerated. Exhausting, disconcerting, frustrating, difficult, but most of all, tediously slow. Marshal Ephraim Tucker had sent along one of his deputies to help Doc. His name was Aaron Fales. Upon being introduced to him shortly before departing Pawnee City, his last name registered in Doc's brain, prompting the hope that that was all that it was, and not an omen. Aaron claimed to be twenty-one, but looked about four days past his sixteenth birthday. He wore a Stetson one size too large for his head, but his prominent ears kept it from sliding down over his eyes. He could ride and he could shoot. He was tireless, willing, and extraordinarily cooperative, but as a conversationalist he was an absolute washout.

" 'Pears they skee-daddled.''

They had located the sod house out at the end of the world south of Eagle. Evidence of the fray was scattered about— broken lances, arrows, dead ponies collecting masses of green flies, blood staining the ground and the front door, the burnt roof, the grass around the house trampled flat, wheelprints from the stagecoach, and the bodies of two white men, one decapitated. To Doc's relief, neither one's build resembled Raider's. Aaron recognized both as Iversons, when Doc suggested that was who they might be.

There was no sign of Raider or Queen Milena, however, he decided ruefully. He could assume that she had been there, but could only guess if Raider had caught up with her kidnappers. And yet, if they were in a stage and he was on horseback, how could he not. Doc shielded his eyes from the sun, scanning the landscape. Was he lying dead somewhere out there with the other two Iversons? He was afraid to search. Aaron looked for him, riding off in an ever widening circle. He reported back twenty minutes later: He had found two more corpses, neither of which fit Raider's description.

"They took her with them, and probably him."

"They was Oglalas, Dr. Weatherbee."

"How can you be sure?"

Aaron held up a long buckskin case decorated with blue, yellow, and black beading.

"This here's a Oglalas' bow case. Been ripped from his quiver. You can tell by the decoratin' an' these here frilly ends."

"*You* can tell." The boy nodded. "You wouldn't know where they might be camped . . ."

"This here's 'bout as fur south as they ever git, ceptin' the Brulés. They're usual up to Powder River country or to the west."

"Oh, dear."

"Findin' 'em shouldn't be hard." He glanced about the

trampled area. "They was some big bunch. They've left us a track a mile wide."

Short on conversational niceties, long on common sense, reflected Doc, conscious of a warm feeling surging through his stomach. Maybe his luck was changing.

"Only one thing," Aaron continued. "We can more'n likely locate 'em okay, but what do we do when we do?"

"We'll worry about that when we find them."

"It's a fair-sized worry, iffn you don' mind my sayin' so." He scanned the sky. " 'Pears like it's gonna rain some. We best get goin' afore their tracks washes out on us."

Milena, who had the freedom of the camp, visited Raider later that day, bringing him a breechclout to replace the blanket. She sat cross-legged opposite him, talking animatedly, gesturing, extolling the virtues of the "noble savage." She kept using the phrase. He frowned. She stopped abruptly.

"What is it?"

"They may be noble to you, but they can be rough as a cob when their dander's up. An' even when it's not."

"You keep saying that. You are worrying unnecessarily. I certainly do not intend to do anything to get their 'dander' up."

"Well, you might start learnin' a little tepee manners. It couldn't hurt none."

"Any."

"None, any, what the hell's the difference? Start by sittin' right."

"You do not think I should cross my legs?"

"It's not what I think, it's He-Dog an' your friend Crazy Horse. Woman's supposed to behave proper inside the lodge. Plains Indians got strict rules."

"How interesting! Such as?"

"If the flap's open an' you're a friend you can come right in. If it's closed you call out afore comin' in. A man comes in, he goes to the right an' waits for his host to invite him to sit in the guest's spot back here to the rear to the left o' the host. A woman always but always comes in after the man. An' goes to the left 'stead o' the right.''

"That is demeaning.''

"For a queen, maybe, but I don' think most o' this bunch even knows what a queen is, let alone that you're one. Somethin' else: When you come to eat you got to bring your own bowls an' spoons. An' be sure you eat every speck they give you.''

"You did not eat your corn.''

"It was rottener than a dead rat. If I'da ate it it woulda killed me. The squaws knew that. It was their idea of a little joke.''

"Continue with the lesson on etiquette.''

"It's not etiquette, it's just good manners. You're never supposed to walk between the fire an' somebody, but walk behind. They'll lean forward to make room. An' I already told you, you don' sit cross-legged. Sit on your heels or with your legs to one side.''

She nodded, but did not change position.

"There's a signal for when you're supposed to get up and leave. The host picks up his pipe an' starts to clean it. That means everybody visitin' gets out.''

"Where did you learn all this?''

"Picked it up. You run aroun' their territory, rub elbows with 'em, you're boun' to pick up a few things. Like worryin' what they're gonna do with us. You can bet they're not gonna feed us an' grin at us much longer. Crazy Horse is scheming something. An' He-Dog's likely feedin' him suggestions.''

"He-Dog does not like you.''

"Black Shawl doesn't like you.''

"She loves my dress and shoes and unmentionables.''

"Don't expect too much appreciation in return. She doesn't need you.''

Milena uncrossed her legs and thrust them out to one side. "What she needs is a doctor.''

"She's got Blue Wolf, the medicine man.''

"She has tuberculosis. He cannot cure her.''

"Don't be surprised. He's tryin'. He's got a lotta tricks. All medicine men do. They sure cure more'n they kill."

"I can help her more than any crude savage."

"If you're smart you'll keep your nose outta it. Keep clear o' her. You can't win in that game. If you did cure her, you'd bust Blue Wolf's nose and there'd be hell to pay. If you didn't, worse, if she died on you, Crazy Horse'd come down on you like a tree. So stay away from her, please."

She shook her head. "She sits in her tepee all day. What she should be doing is sitting in the sun, filling her lungs with fresh air. Exercise is very helpful with tuberculosis."

"You a doctor?"

"I know something of medicine."

"You just got to tamper, right? Stick your nose in, even if it gets you scalped."

"Do you know what your biggest trouble is?"

"You."

"You are a worrier. About everything. A born pessimist. I am just the opposite."

"Three cheers for you."

She was staring at him, making him feel self-conscious. "I must get some water and wash you. It is unhealthy for you to be all smeared with ashes like that."

He-Dog interrupted. Coming in, he gestured for Raider to get to his feet. When Raider failed to move quickly enough, He-Dog jerked him up. Pushing him outside, he tied his hands behind his back even tighter than the squaws had tied them earlier, shoving Milena to one side when she protested.

At the rear of the camp, where the warriors' ponies were tied and the stage stood, a fence fashioned of beechwood had been erected, enclosing a pen about thirty feet in diameter. In the center stood a pole with the shaft of an arrow driven half its length into the top. Pushing Raider ahead, He-Dog walked him up to the fence, tripped him, tumbled him in a heap, and, setting his foot hard against his bottom, shoved him bodily through an opening. Crawling in after him, he got Raider to his feet.

A lariat was tossed to He-Dog. There was a small loop at

the free end. Reaching as high as he could, He-Dog slipped the loop down over the arrow imbedded in the pole. Then he tightened the lariat around Raider's neck.

The rope was about fifteen feet long. He pushed Raider stumbling back to the fence and started him running, pounding him on the back with his fist and pushing him away. Raider loped around the pole while his antagonist crawled back outside. Milena stood in front of the tepee looking on. Everyone in camp quickly assembled outside the fence. Braves and small children climbed up on the stagecoach to watch. Raider pulled up, his heart suddenly beating furiously, the chill, clammy sweat of apprehension breaking out all over him.

The crowd made way for two warriors bringing up a blanket, its four corners tied together. Setting it on the ground by the hole in the fence, they untied the corners, freeing a half-grown panther. They pushed her inside the pen and scurried clear.

Raider froze. The panther, coal black with gleaming yellow eyes, cast about warily. She saw him and ignored him, squatting on her haunches and yawning, shaking her head. She was upwind of him, and the ashes smeared over his body helped mask his scent. But he was sweating. . . . She turned her eyes from him. The onlookers became impatient. Sticks and poles were thrust through the fence, poking at her, goading her. Squaws and children began pelting her with stones. One struck her in the head. She recoiled angrily, snarling, baring her huge teeth dripping saliva.

Again she looked at Raider. He was standing motionless. A pole jabbed her in the haunch. She whirled, snatching hold of it, snapping it like a dry twig. Raider swallowed and bit his lower lip until it hurt. Her eyes returned to him. She started slowly toward him. He began running.

Round and round he ran, the panther loping easily at his heels, the crowd screaming. Breaking out of her circle, she cut him off. He stopped short, twisting, trying to get out of her path. She came straight for him, bounding lightly. He had half turned. Out shot one paw. He yelled; five red slashes

appeared, angling down his calf. The crowd roared approvingly.
Panicking, he began running every which way, trying to keep
clear of her. But the scent of blood had aroused her killer
instinct. Her tongue unrolled over her teeth, thick strings of
saliva dropped from her jaw, a guttural sound escaped her
throat.

The game was changed. No longer was he a moving object
to chase. He was fresh meat, warm blood, nourishment. She
growled savagely as he twisted out of her path.

He was tiring. Her claws had dug deep, and his calf felt as
if a torch was being held against it. He was losing a great deal
of blood; it spattered the ground all over the pen. He flung his
head from side to side absurdly, digging his chin into his
breastbone in a useless effort to loosen the rope. It was so
tight it was cutting off his air. He stumbled. The cat braked,
gauged the distance separating them, and sprang, hurtling
through the air, the single muscle under her shining coat
binding her strength like a coiled spring. Slavering, her fear-
some teeth glistening in the sun, she landed, missing him by
less than a foot. She twisted about, closing on him, snapping,
again missing, roaring frustration.

Bunching her lithe body, she sprang again, catching him
with his right side against the fence. She landed on his back,
sending him sprawling, and fell off him as he dropped,
leaving twin sets of slashes crimsoning his black back. She
landed on her spine, beating the air with her paws. Lurching
to his feet, swaying as he rose, he resumed running.

Again she pounced.

An arrow sang through the air, driving cleanly through her
neck. She twisted in midair, howled in agony, and dropped in
the dust. All heads turned. A brave, standing on top of the
stage, slowly lowered his bow. Directly opposite him, removed from the crowd, standing with Black Shawl by his
side in front of their tepee, Crazy Horse lowered his upraised
arm.

For three days Raider lay on his stomach in front of
He-Dog's tepee. Milena ministered to him in full view of the
tribe, none of whom so much as glanced at them just out of

curiosity. She washed his body and, at his direction, clotted his fifteen wounds with cobwebs and ashes. Luckily, not one of the slashes gave signs of becoming infected; however, this in no way lessened his discomfort. All his new pain only served to overwhelm the discomfort of his swollen shoulder. The rope that had all but strangled him left a burn an inch wide, a great red welt that cast Black Shawl's similar wound into insignificance in comparison.

Milena fed him rabbit stew and edible corn mush. Crazy Horse did not come near him, nor did He-Dog. He was in no mood for a visit from either one. All he really wanted was to sleep. Even eating was difficult for him, since it required him to move his mouth and with it his jaw muscles, which tugged the raw skin on his neck and felt like someone was cutting his throat. Milena was seething.

"Animals! Filthy beasts!"

"No more noble savage?"

"It is not funny!"

"It's sure not. But there's a little silver in the cloud. Think 'bout it. I coulda been killed in there so easy. He stopped the show just in time. Even better, he planned on stoppin' it. Why else plant a brave on top o' the stage? That was some shootin', thank God. Still . . ."

"What?"

"It could be he stopped the show before I bought it just to keep me alive. Hell, all the fun aroun' here stops when I die. This way they can put me on doin' somethin' else real entertainin', once I'm back to walkin' again."

"Not *they*. He-Dog. Crazy Horse did not do it."

"Who knows whose idea it was? Come on, skin, knit. You know I can actually feel each one separate?"

"You are healing. You have lovely scabs. The sunshine is helping. When you are well again I want to get Black Shawl out in the sun. All she does all day long is sit in that foul tepee and cough and cough."

"Let's not start on that again, okay? I'm just not up to wranglin'."

"Do you think you'll be able to walk tomorrow?"

"I can now."

"No, lie still." She placed a restraining hand on his unafflicted shoulder.

"Whatcha got in mind now?"

"We must escape."

"You gettin' bored already?"

"Be serious. We are in grave danger here."

"Oh? Whatever give you that idea?"

"We must leave. I have a plan. It involves the coach. The four horses that belonged to the Iversons are tied separately from the Indians' horses. Tonight, if there is no moon, and it is beginning to become overcast, I will hitch the horses to the coach. I know how to. If you can make it to there I will help you inside and we will get away."

"Just like that."

"I realize it will be risky."

"Risky! It's goddamn suicide!"

"Must you swear?"

"For chrissakes, you won't get within ten feet o' them without at least one settin' up a fuss. They're stallions, they're always makin' noise, 'specially when they get nervous. They hear you sneakin' up on 'em, they'll raise the roof."

"Then I will steal mares," she said stubbornly.

"Theirs? Are you crazy? They're not even broke to saddle, let alone traces and pole. You're not makin' sense. You do somethin' foolish an' they'll scalp you so fast, so slick you won't feel it till you see it in his hand!"

"Nonsense! Crazy Horse would not let any of them harm me, not even He-Dog."

"Like hell. Just forget it. We'll try somethin', somethin' with the littlest possible risk. It's got to be timed perfect, the perfect situation, somethin' goin' on, you know, to distract 'em. The whole pack. I was watchin' Crazy Horse talkin' to old Red Cloud a while ago when you were fetchin' water for me. I couldn't make out a word they were sayin', but Red Cloud kept pointin' north and noddin' his head. It wouldn't surprise me if tomorrow mornin' they all start packin' their travois."

"Why leave here?"

"Who knows? I'm only guessin' they're even fixin' to. Could be they're plannin' to join up with some other tribe. If they go on the move so do we, and while we're movin' is our best chance to get away."

"You are right."

"So will you leave it to me an' not do nothin' rash, promise?"

She nodded, and looked over at the stage longingly. She sighed. "How did we ever get into this?"

"I wonder," he said drily.

CHAPTER NINE

The heavens gave and the world of western Nebraska received. The rain thudded down upon the shake roof of the little office relentlessly, threatening to spring the sides. Outside, the main street dividing Visitation Flats had been reduced to a quagmire. The buildings, dimly seen across the way through a crystal curtain, looked as if they were floating on a pond. Visitation Flats was giving every indication of washing away into the valley to the south.

Inside the office a pie tin set in the middle of the floor rang with the sound of a steady dripping from the ceiling. Doc sat in his underwear, his back to the Sears and Roebuck Bright Sunshine Self-feed Base Burner Stove, his saddlebags at his feet, his clothes suspended from a rope strung from one side of the office to the other. At the far left hung his brand new blue pin-check cotton coat, looking as if it had been dunked in a horse trough and bunched into a ball. Beside it hung his favorite black alpaca vest, as crumpled and shriveled as a well-used handkerchief. Over the stove flew his trousers, from knees to cuffs as wrinkled as a turtle's neck. Next to them hung his shirt, at the moment looking much more like a washrag with buttons, so limp and shapeless was it. But all of these articles, in spite of their sorry appearance and woeful condition, would regain their respective shapes and fashionable features. He was not altogether sure about his curl brim derby. It sat on top of the sheriff's desk, thoroughly wet through, the brim curling in a manner never desired or even considered by the man who had created it, warping out of size and grievously out of fit. The sight of it brought a surge of sadness to Doc's throat. In comparably poor condition, bruised and battered by the rain, dampened and flaccid was his soul within him, he reflected dourly. Aaron and he had covered the last thirty miles under the lash of the rain, thrashed by it, pounded down into their saddles, the sight of the road ahead completely obliterated six feet beyond their horses' nostrils. The horses, bless them both, were now comfortably stabled and drying out. Two more miles, mused Doc, and both would have begun to develop webbed hooves. Aaron, meanwhile, was down the block at the Western Union office, awaiting an answer to Doc's telegram to Marshal Tucker in Pawnee City. Doc had also surrendered to the demands of his conscience and gotten word off to Wagner in the agency's Chicago office apprising him as to where he had gotten to and what he had uncovered so far in the chase after Raider and his royal charge. The wire to Wagner was admittedly a concession to the twin lords of discipline and duty, and Doc was presently entertaining second thoughts over instructing Aaron to send it. When William Pinkerton learned what he was up to he might very well come running with a dozen operatives and six platoons of heavily armed bluecoats. And God help him if the chief got wind of it. Up would go the balloon, taking with it whatever chance he might have of recovering the two captives. On the other hand, somewhere along the way he had to begin going by the book—if for no other reason than to protect himself when the whole dismal mess came to its conclusion.

Seated at his desk was Sheriff Burton Oliver Sedgewick, a pink mountain of flesh, of wheezing, grunting corpulence, of chins and rolls and a belly that put the Bright Sunshine Self-feed Base Burner Stove to shame. Sheriff Sedgewick was amiable and cooperative, and he was the Law in Visitation Flats and the surrounding county. Sedgewick was the baldest human Doc had ever met, there being, after all, degrees of baldness. His almost perfectly round head looked as if it had never supported so much as a single hair in his nearly sixty years. No such encroachment seemed possible north of the man's eyebrows. By the door, his chair tilted against the wall, sat Deputy Lyle O'Hara, a gaunt, bony, unsmiling young man. He was devoutly stupid, decided Doc. He sniffled and whittled and occasionally stuffed his mouth with his harmonica, offering a few baleful passages and then stopping abruptly when the conversation resumed. Opposite O'Hara, leaning forward in his chair, his rough-hewn hands clamped to his knees, his mohair suit infuriatingly dry, sat Hale Stoddard, a trader and antediluvian arrival in Visitation Flats. He had come down the Bozeman Trail, the route to the old Montana gold fields, and was passing through on his way to Topeka to pick up supplies of canned goods, household wares, and other items in scant supply on the frontier.

"Their trail washed out miles back," continued Doc. "The only reason we were able to follow it as far as we did was because they'd brought along the stagecoach and had to stick to the road. Now we've lost them for good."

Stoddard grinned, displaying three isolated teeth—two lowers, one yellowed and rotting but clinging to life in his upper gum.

"Maybe not. You're heading into the Oglalas' home territory—eastern Wyoming, southeastern Montana, and across the borders into South Dakota and Nebraska. With a little luck you ought to be able to catch up with them. Settlers'll see them passing. What you should do is buttonhole everybody you meet."

"Luck is what we'll be needing if and when we do find them," murmured Doc morosely.

"You can thank your stars that young deputy recognized this was Oglala," said Stoddard, holding up the bow case found by Aaron at the sod house.

Doc nodded. Rising, he reached into the pocket of his jacket hanging on the line, bringing out a cheroot. It was discouragingly limp. He held it upright in front of him; slowly it began to bend. Muttering, he tossed it into the stove and banged the door irritably. "You know your Indians. Why do you think they attacked that soddy? They passed up every other place on the way down, as far as we could see."

"It wasn't just a whim. Could be those boys sold 'em rotten whiskey. Or maybe they stole a squaw." Again he showed his teeth. "Maybe practicing up for the kidnapping."

"Are any of the tribes stirring where we're heading?"

"They're most always trying to start something. The direction they seem to be heading they could be fixing to torch Camp Sheridan. The Oglalas are Sioux, and you know how troublesome they can be. Red Cloud, Crazy Horse, and the rest of the war bonnets hate the white man. Hate the Crows, too. Hate just about everybody except their own."

Doc sighed. "The irony of it is my partner could get away from them easily. He's very resourceful. Especially when they're on the move the way they are. But with the woman along . . ."

"Don't be too sure they still got him. I hate to say it, but he could be deader than Balak's bullocks—scalped, skinned, and feeding green flies. Both could be. Captives are excess baggage when the action starts, and the Oglalas never go too long between actions."

"Wouldn't they have some value as hostages?"

Stoddard shrugged. "Maybe. Indians aren't too keen on taking hostages."

Doc reflected on the trader's pessimism, wondering worriedly how Raider was faring. Queen Milena. She had gotten him, gotten them both into this mess. How comfortable and relaxing it had been on the train, living with a king and almost like him from Lawrence to Junction City. Only to have it all blow up in their faces.

Stoddard broke into his train of thought. "You and that partner of yours must be pretty close. You teamed up long?"

"A little over a year now."

"You Pinkertons keep the same partners on every case?"

"Yes. We get used to working together, get to where we can anticipate each other's moves. In a manner of speaking, each of us becomes the other's self."

"Is he educated like you?"

Doc suppressed a smile. "He's from near Viola, Fulton County, Arkansas. He left school when he was ten. He had to. His mother died and his father needed help around the farm."

"Plowboy." Stoddard snickered.

Doc stopped him with a scowl.

"No offense. I come from tiller stock myself; sugarbeeting down the mountains west of Denver. Honorable profession, farming. I guess you must get to be real close friends when you work with a man close as you two have to work."

"Best friends."

"Ever save each other's lives?"

"What exactly is your line? You mentioned household goods."

Stoddard chuckled. "Most anything anybody'll buy, except bad whiskey. I draw the line at poisoning folks."

"Firearms? Ammunition?"

Stoddard's face clouded. The door flew open and banged against the wall, startling O'Hara and all but sending him vaulting from his chair. Aaron came stomping in. He shed his glistening poncho, whipped his hat off and shook it hissing against the stove, and grinned impishly.

"All set. Both wires got off slick as you please." He pulled a crumpled telegram from his pocket, proffering it to Doc. "This here's for you. From Ephraim." He laughed and winked.

Doc read to himself and smiled. The two Montenegrins had decided not to wait around for Judge Gaitenbee after all. Tucker had come to the office one morning and had taken their breakfast in to them only to discover the bars pulled out of the window and the cell empty. Doc told the others.

"That's crazy," scoffed Sedgewick. "No man living can pull iron bars out of a window with his bare hands. They must have been loose."

"They was tight as a trivet," asserted Aaron. "They pulled 'em out, all right, you betcha. Them two boys was strong as Africa gorillas. It took seven full-growed men to arrest 'em and bring 'em in. And in the doin' they beat hell outta the lot of us. Two o' the boys hadn't showed up for work even by the day me and Doc left, right Doc?'' He paused. ''Still, I'm kinda glad they got away. It was all Ozzie Schofield's fault. He's the one should be footin' the bill for the damages to the Pawnee House.''

.Doc felt his clothes. His spare suit was dry, folded neatly in one saddlebag, but he'd be damned if he'd ruin it the way he'd ruined the one he'd had on. He found his trousers dry enough to put back on, wrinkles and all. First chance he got he'd get them pressed, he promised himself, staring down at them. Moving to the door, he looked out into the night, squinting through the rain curtain. There was no sign of a letup. He checked his watch. It was getting on to ten o'clock. He and Aaron could sleep in cells out back and leave early in the morning. Maybe the rain would have let up by then, perhaps even stopped. He sneezed and excused himself.

'You catchin' a cold?'' inquired Aaron solicitously.

''No.''

He knew that he was. Sedgewick did also. Pulling open the bottom drawer of his desk, he got out a bottle and held it up to the lamp. He glared. It was empty. Not a drop. O'Hara lowered his eyes and his head self-consciously and blew up and down the scale on his harmonica. Then he started playing ''Old Dog Tray.''

Before dawn the Oglalas had struck their tepees, packed their travois, and broken camp, leaving the stagecoach and their smoldering fires. Raider and Milena were given two of the stage horses to ride and were placed in the middle of the procession. He would have liked to have gotten back the mustang stolen in Pawnee City, but it was long gone, doubtless appropriated by one of the braves who recognized decent horseflesh when he saw it. One thing was sure, the legitimate owner had to be mighty upset. If he ever got out of this hatful of spiders maybe he should send the poor man a couple of dollars.

His captors had also given him a pair of ancient deerskin trousers and a cotton shirt missing one sleeve whose original owner was no doubt suffering permanently closed eyes. Raider could guess why Crazy Horse would be concerned over what he wore on the move: His fair skin would show up like a beacon.

He felt much improved. His wounds were beginning to knit, and they itched ferociously, especially those chevroning his leg. It was all he could do to keep from clawing the scabs off. He-Dog rode behind him and to the left. Under the skin at the nape of his neck Raider got the feeling that the ugly one wanted them to try to make a break for it. Wanted the distinction of cutting them both down. He was damned if he'd give him the chance. Whatever they attempted, it would be at night, hopefully far removed from He-Dog's snake eyes, hopefully during a storm. It had begun to rain moments after they started out—fat, heavy drops thumping down on his head and shoulders. Only a shower, with no potential for a storm, he thought, likely the edge of one concentrating its fury downstate.

"Why do you think we are moving?" she asked.

" 'Cause the horses' legs are. Who knows? Mr. Feathers never does stick in any one spot too long. Which is why Uncle Sam has so much trouble keepin' 'em on their reservations. Bare feet is itchy feet."

"Are."

"Are what?"

"Are itchy feet."

"Oh for chrissakes!"

"Stop swearing."

"Oh, shut up!"

"Do not be rude." She reached across and laid her hand on his arm. It felt warm and comfortably inviting, snuffing out his ire before it could rise. "I miss you."

"I'm right here."

"You know what I am talking about. I miss having you in my mouth and feeling you inside me. When you are in me and I move I feel the fire all the way up to my throat. It is magnificent. You are magnificent. Tonight we will lock."

"Tonight we will sleep."

"If we cannot lock, if you do not yet feel strong enough to, I will make you hard and fill my mouth with you."

"Please . . ."

"I like that. I love you hard, throbbing. I want to swallow you whole."

As she rambled on in a matter-of-fact tone Raider felt himself stiffening against the front of his trousers. They were old, the skins rotted. Any more out of her mouth and he might split them, come, shoot all over the mare's mane, and set He-Dog laughing so hard he would throw up his breakfast.

"Please knock it off, please . . ."

To his relief she stopped talking, was stopped by Crazy Horse, riding down from the front of the line to confer with He-Dog. They spoke briefly, then Crazy Horse rode back up front.

"What is going on?" she whispered.

"Who the hell knows? It's stopped rainin'."

"Will we stop soon, do you think?"

"Want to know what I really think? We're headin' into Teton Sioux country, just over the border, an' if we stop there, that's good. But if we keep on an' get up into Powder River country on the way to the Big Horns, that's the Crow's backyard. Oglalas an' Crows got 'bout as much love for each other as polecats an' wolves." She smiled. "Did I say something funny?"

"Something helpful. Pray that we do not stop until we reach the Crow yard. If there is a battle, that will be our best chance to escape. Is that not so?"

"That will be our best chance to get killed. If I gotta be in the middle o' shootin', bein' bare-handed I'm kinda what you might call at a disadvantage. As for you . . ."

"Crazy Horse will protect me, and I will protect you."

"Sure. I hate to say it, but you haven't been doin' such a bang-up job up to now."

"You are alive, are you not?"

"Parts o' me is. Do us both a favor. Try an' get this into your pretty head. Sooner or later this bunch is gonna get itself into action. I can see it in Crazy Horse's eyes. If we're still around, we're gonna be right in the thick of it.''

''Will their women and children?''

''They can't help but be if the Crows attack their camp. That's what makes fightin' interestin', catchin' the other fella with his wife an' kids. That's catchin' him in the belly, where it's soft.''

He felt a hand hard on his sore shoulder. He-Dog. He was scowling. He began dressing Raider down loudly and wetly.

''All right, all right, Puke Face. I think he wants us to cut the chatter.''

They rode on in silence surrounded by gossiping, laughing, arguing Indians. They rode for ten suns and rested for eight moons and two cloud-shrouded nights. They rode into and through Sioux territory in South Dakota and on to Wyoming. On the tenth night, camping in the open air without raising their lodges, the braves began looking to their weapons, sharpening knives and tomahawks and their few old cavalry sabers, checking and repairing bows, arrows, and lances, and taking stock of their meager supply of ancient guns. Raider didn't need an indoctrination lecture on the tribe's immediate future plans, but he didn't draw Milena's attention to what was going on. They were fed together and, after they were done, were left to their own devices as usual.

Milena's device was the same as it had been since the fourth night following their departure from the old camp. She wanted satisfying, in quantity, in an uninterrupted display of what had come to be extraordinary sexual prowess on Raider's part. Her lust never seemed to abate, never lessened in the slightest, as far as he could see. It would not have surprised him if she were to approach Crazy Horse and offer to take on every male in the tribe above the age of ten. The woman was incredible. He had known no small number of women who loved sex, any way, with anyone, at any time. But not one could begin to approach either her capacity or her endurance. She was wearing him to a frazzle. Every night followed the same set procedure. They would start out fucking the minute she heard snoring around them. She would then consume him once, twice if it was in her head to do so. This was followed by another "locking," and another immediately after that. Everything they did had to be immediate: no rest for the weary between the acts. She herself never wearied, or at least never showed it. How she could get all that energy out of buffalo stew, corn mush, jerky, and greens was more than he could understand. He ate the same food she ate and nearly twice as much of it, but it imbued him with nothing like the strength and durability she derived from it.

He was losing weight. His ribs were sticking out. What little fat he carried around his neck, waist, and hips was vanishing. Everything on him was getting thinner and thinner, and he constantly felt weak. Still she punished him. It was as if she was bound and determined to make up for all the sexless, sleep-filled nights she had experienced since the catastrophe of her wedding night. Which reflection got him to thinking about Buffalo Bill Nicky. Maybe he wasn't a wash-out after all. Maybe it was deliberate on his part. Maybe, as he saw it, if he gave her an inch she'd take it all, she'd never let up on him, he'd never get another decent night's sleep as long as he reigned. And die of old age at thirty.

"You sure as hell are agin' me," he muttered, easing his limp, reddened, and smarting member out of the trap of her mouth. She swiped the corner of it clean of come, swallowed, licked her lovely lips, and smiled.

"Aging you? How? Surely not by making love."

"Is that what you call this?"

"What do you?"

"Torture."

She laughed. "You are such a tease. Torture indeed! On the contrary, lovemaking is the healthiest, the most beneficial activity there is. The stable master told me that, and he is quite right."

He grunted. "You ever hear o' what folks call moderation?"

"Are you saying that I am too demanding, I overdo it? Nonsense! I do not touch you during daylight. Darkness brings privacy. I am afraid of the dark. I have always been. I need you beside me."

"I'm not aside you, I'm in you!"

"Enough talk. Come, let us lock."

Raider groaned to himself. It was beginning to look as if he'd be meeting his maker either way: at the hands of the Oglalas or hers. Either way he'd suffer.

At least her way he could enjoy it.

Doc and Aaron rode out early and bright. The sun was spreading its gold over the sodden land, drying the puddles in the road, dulling the glistening grasses. Wildflowers bobbed their pretty heads in the gentle breeze wafting down from the distant Rockies. Within the seas of grass stretching as far as they could see on both sides, jumping mice, pocket mice, pipits, sharp-tailed grouse, prairie chickens, and a dozen other creatures foraged unseen, scurrying about after their food supply, the insects, which strove to scurry faster. In the distance two pronghorns bounded lightly across the horizon. They passed a prairie dog town. The creatures began barking, not at sight of them, noted Doc, but some other, unseen invader into their domain, barking and scurrying into the nearest burrows. Fall was only two months away, a time when hundreds of migrating prairie rattlers would converge upon the town to hole up for the winter. Moving into the tunnels, the intruders would coil up and prepare to hibernate. In time, after enough confrontations to discourage them, the poor dogs would pack their resentment and evacuate the area en masse, moving off to build a new town close by. Year after year, back came the snakes to the same denning burrows, but eventually, left untended by the hardworking original owners, the tunnels would collapse and the snakes would move on to take over another town.

In the spring the prairie dogs hosted another foe: Mating pairs of burrowing owls arrived and took over their tunnels. They puffed up their feathers and spread their wings, presenting a formidable adversary to the startled defenders, charging and pecking them until they surrendered the field. Once the dogs had departed, the owls set to work hauling in shreds of buffalo dung to line their new homes for nesting. The old saw was true, concluded Doc, out here at least: It definitely was a dog's life.

Hale Stoddard had advised them to continue on in a north-westerly direction. Ten days' ride would bisect Nebraska and bring them across the border into South Dakota and Sioux territory. But they should keep their eyes peeled along the way. The Oglalas they were seeking could be anywhere between the Holy Road to the south and the South Dakota border, actually. But Stoddard optimistically put their chances as fair to good of sighting their camp somewhere along their present route—only because the shortest distance between Eagle and Sioux territory was the old and reliable straight line.

The trader had been traveling back and forth through Sioux territory, through practically every tribe's territory for six hundred miles in every direction for the past twenty years. And his scalp was still intact. But he knew the chiefs. More importantly, they knew him as both a harmless and dependably generous man. He always made sure he brought with him a supply of trinkets, ribbons, and beads. Pleasing Mr. Feathers was not expensive. Indeed, it was the cheapest life insurance available in the West. On the other hand, if you didn't offer him something, things could get sticky, depending upon his mood of the moment. Doc reminded Aaron of Stoddard's lecture on the subject.

"All we got is this," said the boy, holding up the Oglala bow case.

"Lovely, let me have it." Doc took it and flung it into the grass.

"Whatja do that for? It was a right good souvenir."

"Mmmmm."

Aaron's mild indignation subsided as they rode on into the morning. They encountered no one of any skin tone until late in the afternoon. According to Doc's map, the Talliadad Agency lay approximately four hours' ride ahead. The Indian agent, Everett Schneidermann, was an old and dear friend of Stoddard's, so the trader claimed, and might possibly have some useful information for them.

"Wheels comin'," said Aaron, pointing ahead.

It was a buckboard, so old and ill-used it appeared to threaten final collapse with every new turn of the wheels. It carried an old man and an older woman in a polka-dotted poke bonnet and a calico dress that looked perfect for a nine-year-old. In her gnarled and nut-brown hands she carried a bouquet of blue-eyed grass, spiderflowers, and rabbitbrush. Her traveling companion was busy hauling enjoyment up the ten-inch stem of a corncob pipe. He doffed his straw hat in greeting.

"Howdy, pilgrims." He stopped his mare and they pulled up. "Where be ye heading?"

"As far as it takes us to catch up with a bunch of Oglalas," said Doc.

"Ain't seen no Injuns on this here road, ain't that so, Miz Crawford?"

"Nary a feather, Mr. Crawford."

"They wouldn't be on the road nohow, not 'less they stolt theyselves a string o' Conestogas." He lifted his skinny arm and pointed to the north. "They's a trail up a ways, mile or so. All the tribes use it. This here road goes straight to the Talliadad Agency. Oglalas'd keep clear o' there."

"Is there a cutoff road up ahead to the trail?" asked Doc.

The old man's face cracked in a hundred places as he smiled, smirked. "I swan! Mister, do you figger folks build their roads to connect with Injun trails? Or Injuns make their trails to connect with our roads? Is that what you figger? Where in Jehoshaphat son o' Ahilud you from, stranger, some city?"

Doc touched the brim of his not-yet-thoroughly-dried-out derby in salute. "A pleasure talking to you, Mr. Crawford, Mrs. Crawford. We'll be on our way now."

"See you again sometime," said Aaron politely.

"Which city?" asked Crawford as they passed by. "If I guess it, will you tell me?"

Mrs. Crawford began cackling and slapping her knee.

"Be it Bawston? New York? Cheecawgo?"

Doc ignored him. Aaron tittered, stifling it in the palm of

his hand as Doc glared at him. He tried to get a cheroot out of his pocket. In drying, it had stuck to the lining, and it broke into pieces when he tried to free it. Muttering under his breath, he threw it away.

CHAPTER TEN

The Oglalas camped the following day. The sun sent its rays straight down into Raider's pate, confirming the time. Crazy Horse selected a meadow fringed by a thick stand of willows to one side and gently sloping hills on the other three. This struck Raider as curious. A small army could conceal itself in the trees without so much as a brass button showing. An unfriendly tribe would normally seize on such convenient cover. But Crazy Horse was not stupid. Quite the contrary. Perhaps he figured to *use* the grove, *plan* on it being infiltrated by an approaching enemy force: The grove would absorb them like a sponge absorbs water, and once they were within, the Oglalas could surround them and fill the woods with fire. Raider was quick to note that no one seemed to question the chief's thinking, least of all He-Dog.

No sooner were the lodge hides spread, the tripod main support frames raised and anchored, the other poles added, and the cover set in place and pinned above the door than Raider approached Crazy Horse. The chief was in discussion with He-Dog and Red Cloud and the ancient one, Chief Single Feather, He-Dog's uncle. Raider stood in silence, his eyes discreetly lowered, until Crazy Horse finished what he was saying. Red Cloud and He-Dog nodded when he had done so, then He-Dog glared at Raider and took a step toward him, his hand going to his knife. Crazy Horse stepped between them. He turned to Raider, his expression questioning.

"Chief, you're gonna fight."

A smile flickered at the corners of Crazy Horse's mouth. "What makes you think that is so?"

"I got eyes. I want to fight with you."

"Why?"

"To prove myself."

"And if you do we must let you live, is that it?"

"That's it, me an' the woman."

"The woman will live. She is caring for Black Shawl. She has promised to cure her of her coughing."

Raider sighed audibly. Trying to get people to mind their own business was a little like asking a fire to put itself out, he thought. Leave it to Milena. She wouldn't be satisfied till she got them both scalped.

"Give me back my six-gun and belt and I'll fight shoulder to shoulder with you an' your boys."

"You have a grudge against Seven Knives and his people, the Absaroke?"

" 'Gainst Seven Knives. He killed my brother. Hung him up like the Mandans do the young braves in the Sun Dance. Hooks ripped him to shreds. Skewered him to death, an' he died screamin', you bet."

The smile broke through. "You are a bad liar. If such a thing had happened you would not know of it. For if you were there you would not be here. But I accept your offer. Can you use a bow?"

"I'd prefer my Peacemaker, if you don' mind."

"I am sure you would. But how do I know you would not turn it on my people and kill those watching you so you can escape?"

"I wouldn't leave the woman. I gotta watch out for her."

Crazy Horse studied him for a long time without speaking. Not only was he fair-haired and his complexion pale, noted Raider, but his cheekbones were not high like an Indian's. Not as high as his own. He must have white blood in him, decided Raider. Many Indians did, even chiefs. More important at the moment, in his eyes Raider could see he didn't trust him. But evidently he couldn't resist the challenge.

Also, the idea of an extra hand on his side appealed to him. Slowly he nodded his head.

"You will have your pistol." He grunted. "Your Peacemaker to make war. Our scouts have found the Absaroke." He pointed to the west. "Beyond those trees four hands' journey of the sun catching the earth. But we will not leave until it is setting. You will ride with He-Dog. You will obey his every command."

Raider nodded.

He managed to tell his story to Milena, in spite of her continued interruptions.

"Have you taken leave of your senses!" she exclaimed heatedly. "You must have a touch of the sun. He-Dog will surely murder you!"

"He'll be too busy to bother. He's gonna have his greasy hands full out there. 'Sides, I'll be helpin' the cause."

"You will be killed in the battle."

"I don' plan to be."

"It is not funny!"

She was furious. He had seen her upset before, raising her voice, berating him, but nothing like this. The way her lovely green eyes snapped at him, her slender fingers curling into claws, he began to wonder if she would attack him, scratch him blind, open up his panther wounds, rip his balls off, anything to prevent his leaving.

"It is stupid! Infantile!" she screamed.

"Sssssh, crissakes, keep it down." He glanced furtively left and right.

"You are deliberately separating us. You are throwing away the best chance we will ever get to escape. Their warriors will be gone, with only the women and children—"

"Don' kid yourself, they all won' be ridin' out. Crazy Horse is smarter'n that. He has to leave the squaws and kids some protection."

"I will sit here and wait and you may never return!"

"I will, an' with two scalps in my belt, souvenirs for you." He attempted a grin.

She gaped. "You would not do such a bestial thing."

"How, with a six-gun? Look, there's no point you jumpin' down my throat. I asked to go, he said okay, an' I'm goin'. I can't back out now."

"Our one chance to escape handed us on a silver platter and you deliberately reject it."

"Milena, I know what I'm doin', goddamn it!" He could feel his blood rising in his cheeks, not because of her reaction, but because in his heart he wasn't sure he knew what he was doing. Separation could be disastrous. Once he, Crazy Horse, and the rest were out of sight the squaws could turn on her and flay her alive. Black Shawl wouldn't be up to stopping them. She hardly had strength enough left to get up a cough. Blue Wolf, whose nose Milena was determined to put out of joint, just might decide to put her in her place. He sighed silently. He could come back and find her cold as a catfish.

"Why do you frown? What is the matter?"

"Nothin'." He had been squatting beside her in front of Crazy Horse's tepee. His eyes fell to her ruby ring with the royal seal, her last link with her country and her station. She twisted it nervously on her finger. He got up slowly. "I got to go fetch my iron. 'Scuse me."

"Go, by all means. You must not let me delay you!"

"I'll be right back."

"Do not bother! I shall not be here! I must go and see to Black Shawl. She is my friend. We are becoming like sisters. She needs me. I cannot be bothered worrying about the medicine man. Go, go and help them fight their precious Ab . . . Ab . . ."

"Absaroke. Crows, to you."

The sun was half a gold coin lying on its cut edge when the Oglalas mounted and moved out, displaying the most colorful collection of war bonnets Raider had ever seen. As ordered, he rode with He-Dog, who, from his expression, didn't particularly relish the white man interfering in the red man's squabble. He scowled and seethed, but held his piece. They rode upwards of two miles straight into the sinking sun, pulling up when Crazy Horse lifted his arm. Two outriders had come galloping back to apprise him of something. Raider glanced about. Every brave was armed with every weapon he owned, including coupsticks. What a waste of a hand, he thought. Better a knife or tomahawk than an ornamented stick to touch your enemy to earn a merit point, entitling you to add one more feather to your bonnet. The hawks and eagles became drabber as the Indians became prettier. Among the entire troupe, upwards of a hundred and fifty battle-tested warriors, he counted fewer than a dozen guns, mostly ancient Henrys. He couldn't imagine they had more than fifty rounds of ammunition among them. He had more cartridges than that in his belt. He made a mental note to be extra careful about how and where he aimed when the shooting started. It was his chance to ingratiate himself with Crazy Horse. If he showed up well it just might earn him two tickets to walk.

If Crazy Horse got good intelligence from his scouts as to location, size of the enemy force, and other key factors out of which to develop his attack strategy, he could take the Crows with little risk and next to no casualties. A night attack had to be uppermost in the pale one's scheming mind—catch them by surprise, slaughter them in their squaws' arms before they could rub the sleep out of their eyes. Half could ride through the village and torch it while the other half circled it, prepared to cut down every man, woman, and child who tried to flee.

There were ifs, of course. What if the Crows outnumbered them two, three to one? What if their scouts spotted them coming? What if they pulled half their braves out early, assembled at a safe distance, and rode back in shooting and slashing, catching *them* by surprise?

The Oglala scouts could get only so close even in darkness, not close enough to judge the Crows' strength, not without risking being caught by the village outguards. Mr. Feathers was clever as hell. The U.S. Army in the Military Division of the Missouri, policing half the country between Lake Huron and the Rockies, between Canada and the Gulf, could attest to that. Head to head, the Indian outclassed the white man in every significant respect save two: numbers and firepower.

They continued on. They had gone about fifteen minutes down into a valley when one of the outriders smelled smoke. Crazy Horse gave the order to slow the advance. Not a word: all hand signals, instantly understood by those he instructed. Shortly they came upon the dying embers of a cook fire. The ground was covered with tracks. It was decided that they had been left by herdsmen, indicating that the Crow village was close by.

The Oglalas continued on through the valley, moving cautiously, anxiously scanning the hills on either side, excellent cover for an ambush. The Crows had to know they were coming, reflected Raider worriedly. How could they not? Nobody ever caught any Indian completely off guard, not even another Indian.

The outriders were keeping a good half mile ahead, positioning themselves well out to either side. The moon disappeared behind a cloud, plunging the valley into darkness. Crazy Horse signaled another halt. Everyone dismounted, ate cold jerky, and slept for two hours. It was nearing midnight when they resumed riding. They climbed, deserting the valley, and finally emerged onto a plain. The moon reappeared, draping everything and everyone in a soft, blue ethereal light, but a thickly wooded area ahead of them obscured any view of the horizon. They moved off to the left. Presently they could see a number of lodges standing in irregular order. Slender, barely distinguishable columns of smoke ascended from the openings at their tops. Orange dots were scattered about the ground, the dying hearts of cook fires.

Crazy Horse signaled, spreading fifty of his men out to either side, circling the village. Raider smiled grimly to himself. The chief had read his mind. The remaining warriors held back, their ponies pawing the ground and tossing their heads nervously. They sensed what was to come, he thought, they always did.

A deadly silence hung over the darkened scene. It reminded him of the scary, ominous quiet just before an explosion, ten seconds of holding your breath, feeling your skin crawl up your arms and the hairs on the back of your neck standing up.

Explosion!

Up went the war cry, splitting the night. Hoofbeats rattled the ground, rifles cracked, and a lethal flight of arrows whirred softly through the darkness. The Oglalas charged, sweeping forward in a line that broke like beads on a string when it reached the lodges. Torches flared, fire arrows arced overhead, finding their marks. Buffalo hide caught, flared, crackled loudly.

Flat to the ground, Raider reloaded, squirming, digging knees and chin into the soft earth, wishing wistfully for a ledge or boulder he might more safely scrunch down behind. There wasn't a stone any larger than his hand in sight. He propped himself up on his elbows to resume firing, three shots into the nearest tepee, three more into the one next to it.

He froze, staring in disbelief. Something was very wrong. Like a false note struck on an instrument in the midst of a beautiful passage it came to him. The village was deserted. Not one Crow could be seen. Not so much as a single arrow answered the Oglalas' furious attack.

He stood up. Realization came to him with the swiftness of a bullet finding his flesh. He swore and winced in pain, swallowing so hard it felt as if he'd broken cartilage in his throat.

He knew where the Crows were, what they were doing . . .

"Milena!"

CHAPTER ELEVEN

Schneidermann, the Indian agent in charge at the Talliadad Agency, had been a gracious host and had tried to provide Doc and Aaron with information, but his expertise, such as it was, was Pawnee-oriented; he had neither seen nor heard of any Oglalas on the move through south-central Nebraska.

It remained for Doc and the deputy to locate the abandoned camp by the arduous and time-consuming expedient of wandering all over the landscape on their own. It was the Iversons' transportation that was to come to their aid. From almost a mile distant the stagecoach could be clearly seen, standing abandoned and horseless against the horizon. Reaching it at a gallop, they began inspecting it. Doc got out the Montenegrins' crude drawing of it.

"You sure are a save-all, Doc," commented Aaron.

"It helps on this job."

Comparing the sketch with the Concord was a meaningless exercise, he knew. The important thing was that he was satisfied that this was the stage the queen's bodyguard had seen pulling away from the Pawnee House. It had to be. Indians as a rule did not collect such equipment; they had no use for it. Patently the only use the Oglalas had for it was to carry Queen Milena and Raider to here.

And where were they now? Wherever they'd been taken, why hadn't the stage gone along? As Raider so often said, there was just no figuring how an Indian's head worked.

"What all are we lookin for, Doc?"

"Whatever we find."

"Like what?"

"Don't talk, Aaron, just look."

The front and rear boots were empty, as was the driver's box. There was no strongbox. The window curtains had been ripped off; the squaws had better use for finished leather. They found nothing in the way of a clue to either Raider's or the queen's presence as passengers. They searched the camp. The fires were cold. Ordinarily they would hold their warmth for as long as four days, depending on the thickness of the bed of coals. They examined the pen in which Raider had been chased by the panther, crawling through the opening and walking around inside briefly. Doc examined the dirt, calling Aaron's attention to the dark substance mixed with it, unmistakably blood.

The trail led to the right of the setting sun. They ate and rested and rode on at seven o'clock, following the tracks until nightfall.

They lay in their bedrolls, the fire between them. Since departing Pawnee City Doc had become inordinately fond of Aaron. How could he not like him, so grateful was he for the companionship. But his conscience was beginning to nag him.

"I've been thinking, Aaron. This mess could drag out for weeks. I appreciate your volunteering to help, I'm more grateful than I can tell you, but it doesn't seem right to take you away from your work."

"My work's your work, 'ceptin' I wears me a badge 'stead o' a little ol' card with a eye on it."

"Your jurisdiction is Pawnee County. We're a long way from there."

"You want me to go back?"

"I don't want you to, not for a minute. It just doesn't seem right to deprive Ephraim of your services, particularly with his other two deputies among the walking wounded. What if he suddenly got his hands full of trouble of some kind?"

"He's got badges; he'd just pass 'em out, deputize his poker pals. He's done it afore."

"I suppose he could."

"Would."

"I'm curious. What do you do when you're not chasing down delinquents?"

"Which?"

"Bad apples."

"Mos' anythin': slop the Dufours' hawgs, shovel shit over to Wallace John Friendly's stable, swamp out the bank ever' other night after closin', mostly clean-up chores. I dugged and fitted a well for the Widow Coates back April."

"Where did you learn to ride and shoot?"

"School o' hard knocks. Teacher Tucker."

"You're good."

"Thankee. Doc?"

"Mmmmm."

"You don' much like saddle, do you?"

"Not much. Nature didn't endow me with the necessary padding. I'm accustomed to a well-upholstered wagon seat. A wagon's slower going, of course, but considerably more comfortable. I find it so. Do you have family back in Pawnee City?"

"Now. Not afore. I was a orphan. Maw died when I was borned. My daddy hung hisself when they tolt him. I was raised in the orphan 'sylum at Lincoln. I learnt how to read an' write an' cipher. I met Uncle Ephraim when I was fifteen. He's got him a couple hunnerd acres an' a apple orchard. Bunch o' us hired out to work for him. He took a shine to me and 'dopted me. All legal an' ev'ythin'. That's how come I call him Uncle. Treats me like blood kin, he does, calls me son."

"Good man, Ephraim."

"Salt o' the earth. Honest, straight as a die. Most respected man in Pawnee City, you betcha."

In the distance a coyote bayed, a long, plaintive cry addressed to the full moon.

"Purely despises religion."

"He does?"

"Somethin' fierce. Calls preachers Bible-beatin' billygoats, hippycrits, holier-as-thous. Don' b'lieve in God nohow; don' b'lieve in nothin' he can't see an' feel. At the 'sylum they give us kids religion like sulphur an' m'lasses for tickly throat, jus' shoved it down us. Mornin', noon, an' night. Sundays was church all day, you betcha. When I comed to live with Ephraim an' Aunt Lillian Gay very firs' day she seen my Bible an' tooked it from me an' hid it in the bottom drawer o' the chest. She says to me, don' let your Uncle Ephraim see that there, he'll toss it down the dry well. She goes to church, he don'; they argues somethin' scand'lous 'bout it. She's afeerd he's goin' to hell when he dies, you see. He tells her he can't wait; says he'll sure 'nough favor the company he'll be akeepin' down thar over the puckered-mouth, stiff-necked do-gooders an' holier-as-thous up to heaven. Claims he knows where the straight an' narrow is just as good as any Jack in the pulpit. He's a caution. They carry on like two bobcats in a burlap bag, you betcha. I near bust my buttons tryin' to keep a straight face. I'm lucky, Doc, luckiest state ward 'live. Life with them sure 'nough beats grays an' beans."

"What are grays?"

"Uniform. Like a uniform. Gray cotton shirt in summer, gray wool in winter. Gray denim trousers all year round. Black ten-button shoes. Keep 'em shiny as a new dime. Were you a orphan?"

"No, I have a father and a mother. They live back east."

"Both. I swan! That is the berries, that is. I ne'er did have a frien' with both. Alton Leacock down at the stable got a daddy but no maw. An' Julia Frye got a maw but no paw. All my other frien's got neither one. Sure is somethin', havin' both. Both healthy?"

"Both healthy."

"You ever get back to see 'em?"

"I plan to, after this mischief is wound up."

"I swan, you sure do talk pretty. Where'd you learn to?"

Doc chuckled. "Boston, cradle of liberty, home of the bean and the cod, Athens of New England."

"How come you got into the Pinkertons?"

"Good question. I guess you could say I was looking for something."

"You found it?"

"Not yet."

"I did. I got ev'ythin' I want an' need back to home in Pawnee City."

"You're a lucky man, Mr. Fales."

"I got me a lil gal, too. Julia Frye. She's purty as a posy. I got a tintype o' her right here."

Both edged toward the fire. Doc blew the flame to life as Aaron got Julia Frye out of his wallet. She had the most innocent eyes Doc had ever seen. She wore her blond hair in pipe curls and appeared to be trying a smile on for the first time, being very tentative about it, afraid she might crack her pretty cheeks.

"She's real shy."

"She's lovely. You sure are a lucky man."

"You betcha. You go steady?"

"Oh, no. Not much chance to go steady, develop any kind of relationship, moving around like Raider and I do."

"You'll settle down some day."

"I expect I will."

There was a long and trenchant pause. The flame died. An ember buried deep in the fire hissed and crackled and was silent. The coyote bayed.

"You thinkin' 'bout him?"

"Mmmmm."

"Don' worry 'bout him. We'll find him, an' that there queen lady too." He yawned and stretched. "Man, I am beat to bones. G'night, Doc, pleasan' dreams."

"Good night, Aaron."

Presently Aaron was snoring contentedly, no doubt, thought Doc, dreaming sweet dreams of Julia Frye. He thought about Raider. On the bright side was the fact that they were on his trail, at least headed in the right direction, roughly. Which was about all there was on the bright side. He was in deep trouble, providing he was still alive, possibly the toughest spot he'd ever been in, drawn into it by Milena and his responsibility for her safety and welfare. Indians didn't read newspapers or look at wanted dodgers on sheriffs' and marshals' bulletin boards. Five thousand pictures of Queen Milena, fifty thousand, could flood the territories and wouldn't help anybody locate her. The tribes were islands of native culture, isolated pockets of people untouched by the white man's influence, almost continually on the move, making them difficult, often impossible to follow, to catch up with, and even more difficult to deal with if and when you did. How could the two of them survive in such a perilous and hostile circumstance? Resourceful as Raider was, it would be difficult. White captives did survive, of course, but they were a discouragingly small minority, and generally only when they found themselves in the hands of tribes less bloodthirsty than any of the Sioux. The Pawnee were cannibals. Virtually every tribe practiced torture as either a test of manhood or for entertainment. The squaws were a vicious lot, eager to abuse prisoners to put on a show for their men. Milena was no delicate flower; she was tough-minded, resolute, spirited, but scarcely less vulnerable than any other woman, any human. Worse, her presence on the scene had to make Raider extremely vulnerable.

There was one other small optimistic aspect to the thing; Neither one was guilty of any offense against the Oglalas. They had just happened to be in the wrong place at the wrong time.

Why had the Oglalas moved out? Out of fear of reprisal for massacring the Iversons? Hardly. It was much too early to stop hunting buffalo. Why leave? Could it be that Crazy Horse was going looking for trouble? Possibly. If that were so, how it would affect Raider and Milena he could only guess. It certainly didn't lessen the danger they were in.

Being an Easterner and educated, Doc had a liberal attitude toward the red man. Emigrants were stealing his lands; the federal government made and broke treaties with the chiefs; injustice, duplicity, and ruthless treatment prevailed. All the tribes were fast traveling to the shades of their fathers, toward the setting sun, though not fast enough for the settlers moving in. The Indians were bitter. Some resisted with uncompromising ferocity; others, the fervent idealists, tried desperately to avoid war with the white man. But the end of their dominion over the lands and the herds was at hand. Doc could sympathize with their plight, and considered the actions of the government and of his own people uniformly shabby and dishonorable. But his feelings on the subject were more or less confined to the abstract.

Raider's and Milena's capture supplanted the abstract with the concrete. Doc pitied her, despite the fact that she had only herself to blame. For Raider he also felt compassion, and with it a sense of abject helplessness, the like of which he had never known. If Crazy Horse killed him he would retaliate; he would take an eye for an eye. He would become John Chivington, the slaughterer of Sand Creek, William Fetterman, and all the other renowned Indian haters rolled up in one personality. His capacity for hatred would become boundless, his hunger for vengeance insatiable.

"I'll kill every red bastard I see!" he burst out.

Aaron stirred, snorting lightly, licking his lips. Having raised himself on his elbows, Doc sank back and closed his eyes. Again the distant coyote raised its baleful song.

Crazy Horse had covered himself with glory on frequent occasions. This time he had covered himself with shame. His enemy had cunningly deceived him. How the Crows had learned that the Oglalas were coming after them wasn't important. They had, and they had turned the tables. All Oglala eyes were on Crazy Horse's stony face when the war party rode out to return to camp. He-Dog had confronted Raider and seized his Peacemaker before ordering him up on his pony. He had not demanded his belt with forty cartridges remaining. This surprised Raider, for all the good shells without a weapon to fire them would do him.

They did not hurry back. Why bother? Every man among them knew what had happened. Raider could see it in their eyes. They knew the Crow mind on the warpath. His way of thinking was a queer blend of cruelty, vanity, greed, foolhardiness, and incredible courage. After victory in battle, after a successful raid they cruelly tormented their helplessly wounded enemies before butchering them. Two days later they would beat the mangled corpses until they collapsed in exhaustion. Male captives were usually hanged by the ankles; the braves would shoot at the victim while their women jabbed him with sharp sticks.

The lot of captive women was much easier. They were generally married to Crow braves and required to perform the usual feminine tasks. Children too were spared.

So Milena was probably still alive, unless she'd taken a stray arrow in the raid. The skeleton guard left by Crazy Horse would be slaughtered, that he would bet on. Knowing what had taken place back at camp in their absence, seeing it clearly pictured in his mind, it seemed a woeful waste of everybody's time to ride all the way back. Still, he had to be absolutely certain she had survived. And if he couldn't find her body, the chances were she had.

He had to find her, and as quickly as possible. He had to get away from Crazy Horse and his people. Riding along half a pony length behind He-Dog, he could see only the corner of his eye, but he could imagine what was going on behind both his eyes. He and Crazy Horse both knew *he* knew what had happened back at camp. Both knew he'd want to get away, just as surely as they'd known before that he wouldn't attempt it, encumbered as he was with her.

He'd just have to play his cards very close to his buttons. Damn, but he'd love to get his Peacemaker back from He-Dog. When they got back to camp he would ask Crazy Horse. The worst he could do would be to refuse him. He was mulling over the possibilities for the twentieth time when they passed a huge uprooted willow marking, as he recalled, a point approximately two miles from the camp. Beyond the fallen tree was a swamp. To his surprise and chagrin He-Dog heeled his pony forward, veering to the left. He snatched the Peacemaker out of his belt and threw it into the swamp.

"Son of a bitch," muttered Raider. Of all the stupid moves. He-Dog's idea of a joke. He turned and smirked at Raider. Crazy Horse had watched him dispose of the gun without saying a word. He obviously had other things on his mind. Check-reining his temper, Raider answered He-Dog's taunting expression with a forced smile.

The stink of death hung over the camp as they approached. The Crows had not torched the lodges but had evidently circled the area, pouring in arrows and gunfire, cutting down the braves remaining behind to protect the camp. Scalped and otherwise mutilated braves' corpses lay about. They found two dead squaws, but the others, the children, and the ponies left behind were nowhere to be seen. Not a single dog was found wandering about, although a number of dead ones were visible. Unlike other tribes, the Crows did not eat dogs. There was no sign of Red Cloud's corpse, but this did not surprise Raider. No one in camp, not even Black Shawl, was a more valuable prisoner. They found Blue Wolf with a knife hilt-deep in one eye.

The Crows' tracks led north. They evidently had no intention of returning to their camp and thereby chancing a meeting with the Oglalas. Raider knew that there were three divisions of the Crow people. Those along the lower Yellowstone, roaming as far as the Missouri confluence, were called River Crow. The two others, the Main Body, *acarahō,* and the Kicked-in-Their Bellies, *ērarpīō,* were Mountain Crow; they wintered in the country of the Wyoming Shoshone, the Wild River region, and ranged from the site of Buffalo, Wyoming, in the Bighorn Mountains to the Pryor district in the spring. Others frequented the territory by the Tongue River in the east and near Livingston in the west. But the Mountain Crow often wandered this far south, invading the hunting grounds of the Cheyenne and Arapaho and even daring to trespass on Sioux territory in the southwest corner of South Dakota.

Crazy Horse and He-Dog were parlaying. Raider got the impression, standing beside his pony watching them, that they would lose little time in getting on the Crows' trail and tracking them until they caught up. Crazy Horse had lost face with his followers, and uppermost in his mind had to be reclaiming it. As soon as possible. Rescuing Red Cloud would help. The old chief was even more important than Black Shawl.

Raider pondered the situation. Should he try to get away and go looking for the Crow on his own? Or should he stick with the Oglalas? If it came to hand to hand, which it eventually had to, it could turn into a bloodbath with Milena smack in the middle.

"And me," he muttered dejectedly.

There were other aspects to consider. If he *were* able to get away he could get to the nearest town and wire Kansas City. On second thought, with what? He didn't have a red cent in his pockets, didn't even have pockets. Then too, Doc had to be long gone from there by now. He squatted by a dead cook fire and, clearing his head of both his concern over Milena and his exhaustion, put himself in his partner's place. It had been more than two weeks since Milena had spirited him away from the train near Junction City. By now Doc had to be on their track, though how he'd manage to get on it was a mystery. Still, that much he had to take for granted. So how far behind was he? Had he reached the old campsite? How many guns did he have with him? How was he tracking them? And who else was? Knowing Doc Weatherbee and his annoying penchant for going by the book, he would most certainly have contacted Chicago by now. What then was Allan Pinkerton up to? Had he called in the Army? What about the Secret Service? You could hardly leave that bunch out. The various possibilities leaped to mind thick and fast, but one after another he dismissed. Doc was his sole concern. Alone or with help, he had to be close behind. If he was smart, and he was. If he used his smarts he'd be following the Indian trails, knowing that the Oglalas would favor them and that even if a torrential downpour washed away their tracks he'd still stick to the trail.

What he should have done was *leave a trail on the trail* for him, hares and hounds. Using what for paper? No. What he really should have done was rescue her as soon as the Iversons reached the soddy, before they even settled in.

He should have. He recalled that he'd been tempted to try, but then put the thought out of mind. Too risky, too ridiculous.

Would he ever see her again? Seven Knives and his people were Mountain Crows and looked to be heading for the Powder River country, Crazy Woman Creek, and the Bighorn Mountains. If he was going to catch up with them it had to be before they reached home.

He-Dog broke into his thoughts, grunting behind him, jabbing him in the back with his knee. Crazy Horse wanted to talk. He was upset over the disappearance of Black Shawl, Raider surmised, studying the chief. In the eyes of his warriors he couldn't risk losing any more face. He was still in charge. Nobody, at least at the moment, appeared interested in taking his bonnet from him. Not with He-Dog around. He was a pain in the neck, abusive and stupid, reflected Raider, but loyal to Crazy Horse, and the chief was in no danger of losing his authority as long as his brother-friend stayed healthy. Then too, every chief had his occasional setbacks. Crazy Horse would make his comeback: by rescuing Red Cloud, Black Shawl, and the rest of the women and children and separating Seven Knives from his hair.

Crazy Horse addressed him. "We will rest here, then we will ride out after the dung eaters. You will ride with us." Raider nodded, mildly surprised. Crazy Horse appeared in no rush to catch up with the raiders.

"The white woman is alive."

"I hope."

"She is. We will rescue all our women and children." He was trying very hard to appear blasé about the situation, Raider noticed, treating it as a temporary setback that would soon be corrected. But his eyes continued to betray his embarrassment.

What made the Crow strategy so clever was that they had given the Oglalas no choice but to ride back to check the camp. They could have assumed what had happened, but Crazy Horse chose not to, as Raider himself would have chosen, had it been up to him. But returning had consumed valuable time. And going nearly seventeen hours with only a couple hours' sleep, making it necessary to rest a second time in order to be fit to fight, not to mention take time to build funeral scaffolds for their dead, would give the Crows a substantial lead. Curiously, none of the Oglalas appeared concerned over the delay.

Crazy Horse's offhand observation that Milena was alive accomplished one thing: It made up Raider's mind. She had to be, he thought, and would continue to be for the foreseeable future. Crazy Horse could not risk a frontal attack when he did catch up with the Crows. Seven Knives held all the cards. The Oglalas had to concoct a strategy clever as hell to turn the tables so cleverly turned on them.

Perhaps Milena would not be in as grave danger as he first thought. If she didn't try anything foolish maybe she was in no danger at all.

And so it was, as Crazy Horse rambled on, describing how weak and vulnerable the raiders were, how capable his warriors, how easy it would be to defeat the dung eaters, that Raider decided he would make a run for it. And back-trail in the slender hope that he would run into Doc and whoever was with him. Hopefully, three hundred bluecoats. He would stick with the Oglalas until they started out, maybe for the first couple miles, then cut and run. It would be the last thing either Crazy Horse or He-Dog would expect him to do—desert Milena at this stage of the game. With a little luck he might be able to catch them off balance just long enough to get clear. If he did manage it they probably wouldn't bother to chase him very far.

Yes, definitely: Cut and run and look for Doc until he found him. He'd have money, guns, ammunition, everything he needed. His hand crept to his empty holster as Crazy Horse rumbled on. The chief noticed the move and paused.

"You miss your Peacemaker."

"Throwin' it away was dumb."

"I ordered him to."

"Why? Didn't I pitch in an' help?"

"What choice did you have?"

"That's not the point."

"Of course it is the point. Unbuckle your belt and give it to me."

"What for? What good is it? You got no .45 caliber iron."

"You have none either. What good is it to you?"

Crazy Horse smiled for the first time in a long time. The hell with it, thought Raider.

Day followed day with monotonous regularity for Doc and Aaron. Taking Mr. Crawford's advice, they followed the Indian trail, climbing into the hills and crossing the White River and the border into South Dakota and Cheyenne, then Sioux territory. Both rode with small knots of fear solidly imbedded in the backs of their necks. All they needed, mused Doc ruefully, would be to run into a roving band of any Indians high on fire water or low on tolerance for white skin. They'd find themselves in trouble as deep as Raider's and the queen's.

On two occasions they spotted parties far ahead. Both times they fled the trail, hiding and holding their breaths until the Indians passed. Doc was meanwhile rapidly descending into a morass of pessimism, which for him was totally out of character. They were chasing shadows, he decided. Logic and common sense both dictated that Raider and Milena were dead, scalped, and their bodies left in a buffalo wallow a hundred miles back. Both were baggage the Oglalas didn't need, no tribe on the move needed.

The sun was high, approaching its zenith, bleaching the land rendered arid and lifeless in appearance by the summer heat. It hadn't rained for more than a week, and around them it looked as if it had been months. Dust prevailed, cloaking everything, stirred by the horses' hooves, rising in thick clouds, invading their clothes, their eyes, nostrils, and throats, even their saddlebags.

"You gettin' down, Doc?" asked Aaron apprehensively.

"The odds in favor of success seem to be getting longer

and longer. We could ride all over creation for the next ten years and not find them.''

Aaron smiled grimly, removing his one-size-too-large Stetson and swiping his brow with the back of his forearm. ''We're overdue a change in luck, don'tcha think?''

''I'm not much of a believer in luck.''

''I believe powerf'ly in it. I figger things can go bad for a feller only so long afore they does a turnabout. That's what's gonna happen with us. Allus works that way for me.''

''Always?''

''Allus. You superstitious?''

''Not so you'd notice it.''

''I am, allus will be. Julia Frye is. On her thirteenth birthday she hid in the closet all day.''

''You're kidding.''

''Honest Injun. Never come'd out onc't. Never et a speck. Nothin' all day. Got to the next day 'thout harmin' a hair on her haid.''

''How about the three hundred and sixty-four after that?''

Aaron gaped.

''Aaron, if her thirteenth birthday was unlucky, why wasn't the whole thirteenth year?''

''''Twere.''

''What happened?''

''Her paw was kicked in the haid by a mule an' died. She busted her arm fallin' outta a tree. Her maw took sick with the dropsy. Their barn was lightnin' struck an' burnt down. The cow died . . .''

''All right, all right.''

''One of their sows took sick an' died o' the fever. Julia's Aunt El come down with the prickly heat somethin' fierce, near scratched hersel' to death. The well run dry . . .''

''Okay, that's enough. I hate to say it, but I think we may be making a big mistake following the trail.''

''It's what the Oglalas is follyin'.''

''No doubt, but white people don't, and we're at least a mile from the main road, well out of sight of anyone traveling it who might be able to give us information.''

"If they're travelin' the road they ain't travelin' the trail, ain' that so?"

"Aaron . . ."

"If they're travelin' the road they wouldn' see no Injuns."

"There are a lot of places where they could, where the hills or trees don't interfere with the sight line." He reined up. "I say we get back on the road."

"You're the boss."

"Let's go."

He cut off the trail heading south. Aaron followed.

Raider played it as safely as he could. It was dusk, and the war party pursuing the Crows was fording a stream when he spotted his chance. On the opposite side the grass rose as high as his pony's back. The stream bank ascended to a group of hills about a hundred yards off to the right. The thick grass would slow his pony, and who could say what the footing was underneath, but it was past time he got away. Crazy Horse and He-Dog would never expect him to try. He just might confuse them, at least enough to delay their reaction. Neither would hesitate to kill him or order him killed, he was sure. Neither one was in any frame of mind to put up with his shenanigans, but it was now or not at all.

He-Dog started across, stopped, and turned, beckoning him forward. Raider scanned the opposite bank. All but one of the braves carrying Henrys had already crossed. The odd man was behind him, but well behind, at the trail of the pack; he had noticed moments before. He nodded to He-Dog and rode up alongside, then ahead of him. He could hear him following through the shallow, slowly moving muddy water. Heeling his mount, he sent it pounding up the bank and into the sea of grass. The pony was war-bridled, the lark's-head knot tightened around its lower jaw, forming the bit. Jerking the bridle would be painful, he knew, but he had to turn the animal fast, and so he pulled hard. It swung right, heading for the hills. A cry went up behind him. Arrows whizzed by. The pony stumbled, and its back legs gave way. Down went Raider, the pony nearly catching and snapping his left leg at the knee. He pulled it free just in time. An arrow had found the pony's haunch, burying six inches deep. The animal whinnied in pain. Raider righted himself and ran. So thick was the grass he couldn't see the ground. It dragged at his legs, slowing him. He ran in a crouch, zigzagging, his head below the grass top.

An arrow sped by his ear so close it nearly took it away. He dove behind a rock and, bouncing back up, began threading his way through the hills. They had stopped shooting and yelling. His heart surged. He'd made it! Still he ran, until his legs and lungs gave out. He stumbled and fell. Rolling over on his back, he studied the darkening, cloud-strewn sky overhead. And listened. He could hear no sound of them. Suddenly he was aware of pain, apart from the stabbing in his chest as he gasped and fought to fill his lungs. His feet. They were drenched with blood.

"Shit!"

He pulled up to a sitting position and examined them. They hurt fiercely, but he could stand it. They would clot. He wouldn't bleed to death. He got gingerly to his feet.

"Son of a bitch!" Gritting his teeth, he ignored the pain, turning his thoughts to his situation. No moccasins, no food or water, no iron, no money, nothing but his disreputable-looking trousers and the one-armed shirt that was beginning to stink it was so filthy. He was in great shape for a hundred-mile walk.

But he was alive, at least for a while. Was Milena? She had to be.

"Just keep tellin' yourself she is, you asshole!"

Doc roamed between the trail and the road, slowing their forward progress, but gaining them two encounters with passing settlers they otherwise would have missed. They passed a lone man late that afternoon and a man, his wife, and eleven children riding a box-brake wagon with a thimble box pulled by four horse wearing fly nets just before noon the following day. The lone pilgrim and the elders of the family agreed that they had seen Indians passing through at just about the time the Oglalas should have passed. Neither had noticed any prisoners, man or woman. No, it was neither a war party nor a hunting party: It was everybody, dragging travois loaded with wants and needs.

Two more days passed. They stopped on the trail, cooked and ate, and were preparing to turn in for the night when Aaron, leaving the fire to check the horses one last time, caught sight of a man stumbling toward them.

CHAPTER TWELVE

Raider was in poor shape, exhausted almost to the point of delirium and half starved: He had been surviving his ordeal on bark and berries. His feet were blackened with bruises and dirt, heavily scabbed and swollen. To Doc he looked as if he had stumbled back from the dead. They fed him and gave him fresh water and it seemed to perk him up, at least enough to stir his dander.

"Where in red hell you been?" he grumbled. "Some partner, some friend. I been at death's door a dozen times since Pawnee City, been starved and beaten, clawed by a panther, poisoned, shot at, shit on, tortured, my shoulder near busted, both feet busted . . ."

"For heaven's sakes, stop griping. You're alive. Be grateful we came along."

"You didn't goddamn come along! You was sittin' here like two toads on a rock. *I* come along."

"Have it your way. Rade, this is Aaron Fales, Marshal Tucker's deputy from Pawnee City. He volunteered to help. He's been indispensable."

Raider shook his hand. "Thanks, Aaron, for getting Mr. Flasharity here this far. He sure as hell couldn't do it on his own."

"Thank you, Rade. Where's Queen Milena?"

Raider told his story. Doc and Aaron listened intently without interrupting.

"I musta come at least two hundred miles on foot," Raider concluded.

"Forty or fifty anyway," interposed Doc.

Raider talked through his comment, not even according it a wave of dismissal. "I weighed the whole situation an' figured it made no sense tryin' to rescue her alone, not without a damn gun. Without even a penknife. Without even boots."

"Let's get one thing straight," said Doc. "Where is she now?"

"Who knows?" snapped Raider irritably. "Gimme some more o' that sludge you call coffee. Crissakes, you never will learn how to make it decent."

Aaron refilled his cup.

"The Crows got her up in Bighorn country."

"But you just said Crazy Horse was on his way to rescue them. That was three days ago. I have a question, a very important one. Rade, how do we know whether he's succeeded or failed? *How do we know who has her, the Crows or the Oglalas?*"

Raider lowered his cup slowly and stared at his partner. He was right, he thought, there was no way they could know. Jesus, how could he have been so stupid! How could he overlook that. It was so important and so obvious.

"How could you overlook such a thing? It's as plain as the nose—"

"All right, all right!"

"By now Crazy Horse must have caught up with them. There was a showdown, one side won, the other lost. But which? Who do you think?"

"How in hell should I know?"

"Which would you bet on?"

"The Crows. No, the Oglalas."

"Make up your mind."

"The Oglalas. The Crows outnumber 'em maybe, and they know they're comin', but Crazy Horse has got to come out on top. He's smart as hell. He's proved it over and over."

"I wouldn't exactly classify the Crows as stupid. They certainly outfoxed him. What makes you think they won't do it a second time? Rade, how in heaven's name could you cut and run before you were certain who is or will be holding her captive?''

"Doc, for chrissakes . . ."

"You blew it.''

"I didn't!''

"You didn't blow it.''

"SHUT UP! Quit rubbin' it in.'' He sipped and stared into the darkness. A squadron of fat blue clouds were moving slowly by above, heading toward the Rockies. The wind sang mournfully, tearing the cook fire flame, nearly extinguishing it. Doc's stallion whinnied. "What do we do, Doc?''

"How can we 'do' anything?'' His tone was tinged with exasperation. "This is going to be like looking for a needle in two haystacks.''

"Just one. The Oglalas got her back, Black Shawl, the lot.''

"We'll just have to go about it the hard way. Do you think the Oglalas will eventually come back to their camp?''

"Hell, yes. You know Indians, they hang onto everything they own long as they can. Why shouldn't they come back?''

"Then you show us the way and that's where we'll head.''

"Not this old boy, not till I can walk.''

"You can ride. We'll get you a horse.''

"And a gun.''

"I have a Winchester. You can have my .38 Diamondback.''

"Gun, not peashooter. And I'll need boots, a saddle . . .''

"We'll get you everything.''

"Lemington comin' up,'' said Aaron, "'bout five mile up the line.''

"We'll fit you out when we get there, Rade, and I'll wire Wagner. The chief must be back from Washington by now. We're going to need all the help we can get.''

"We could cut over to Fort Gunther and get the Army,'' suggested Aaron.

"Fuck the Army,'' snapped Raider. "Turn those bastards

loose and they'll gum up the works for fair. Shoot up a storm, kill everythin' in sight, includin' half their own, goddamn trigger-happy assholes!''

Raider persisted in arguing heatedly against bringing in outside help. He was also dead set against Doc contacting the agency in Chicago, and when his partner admitted that Wagner had already been informed he crabbed and cursed and carried on in a performance that attracted the attention of half of Lemington. He was only striving to relieve his frustration, Doc knew. He had seen him behave so many times.

While Raider was buying a horse and saddle, Aaron and Doc sent wires from the Lemington Western Union office— Aaron to Marshal Tucker, Doc to Wagner and Allan Pinkerton.

A recent fire had burned away almost the entire corner of the office behind the stove. The smell of burnt wood vied with the telegraph operator's bay rum. The man resembled a chicken in too many respects to overlook the comparison: a beaklike nose, skinny neck, elbows positioned and protruding like wings, and a walk, back and forth behind his counter, that jerked his head comically with every step. Doc did not bother to encode his messages to Chicago. In separate tele-grams to his two superiors he detailed the situation to date, closing with the presumptuous assurance that Her Highness would be rescued before the week was out.

"How can you be so sure?" asked Aaron worriedly.

"I'm a firm believer in the power of optimism. The worst we can do is fail. Look at it this way: Neither tribe has any intention of killing her. Indians rarely kill women captives. When we do catch up with whoever's got her we'll talk it over and work out an arrangement.''

"'Rangement?''

"Aaron, if Crazy Horse or the Crow chief doesn't turn her over he can expect a visit from the U.S. cavalry. I can't imagine any tribe willingly inviting unnecessary bloodshed. All things considered, I see no reason why we can't get her back, return her to her husband, and wash our hands of the whole mess.''

Aaron shrugged.

"You think that's wishful thinking?"

"It's a whole lot brighter than Mr. Raider sees it."

"Mr. Raider sees everything as black as it can get."

"May be, but he's in on it."

"Pay no attention to him. As long as I've known him he's been carrying on like six days of rain, whatever the odds or chances. The man never sees the sun."

"You said him and you was friends."

"We are."

Again, Aaron shrugged.

"You think because we argue we don't like each other?"

"Argue? You snap like two dogs over the same bone."

"It's not that bad, it's just that he's down in the dumps. Rade only feels comfortable when he's on top of things, in control. This business is on top of him."

"We're sure 'nough wastin' time hangin' roun' here."

"We have to get a reply from Chicago before we make our move."

The telegraph key clicked, then went dead. The chicken smiled, his inexpensive and ill-fitting teeth slightly awry in his mouth. He deftly straightened them.

"Patience, gents. Your messages got to get through Omaha, then on to Chicago. Takes time. Rome wasn't built in a day."

The door opened. In came Raider, resplendent in a new Stetson, new clothes, new Middleton boots. He walked, noted Doc, as if he had two walnuts in each boot. He had shaved and bathed. A little sorrel with a busily swishing tail was tied outside at the hitch rack.

"What's the holdup, Doc?"

"Just waiting for Wagner and the chief to get back to us. It won't be long."

"Back with what, the usual bullshit?"

The operator sucked in his breath sharply, cleared his throat, and indicated a sign: "NO SWEARING, THE LORD HAS EARS." Raider stared at him with a look calculated to shrivel him in his shoes and went on.

"Bullshit, pure an' un'dulturated. You really think either o' them or anybody back there is gonna help us deal with this mess? The old man'll likely want us to hook up with the local sheriff, get him to ride in with us and arrest Crazy Horse on a charge o' breach o' the peacepipe or whatever."

The operator grinned. Aaron laughed lightly. Raider froze him in mid-titter with a steely stare.

"Rade, one day, hopefully, you'll get it into your head that we don't operate on our own. We're members of an organization. We have superiors. They instruct us. In any organization it's customary, it's necessary to go by the book."

"Fuck the book!"

The operator cringed, shrinking into a tight mass of pain. The key rattled.

"Message coming in," he said, his tone offended.

The key continued speaking. He wrote down the message and handed it to Doc. Raider and Aaron read it over his shoulders.

"I knew it!" sputtered Raider. "Ring in the blue boys. Start a goddamn war while we're at it, get her head shot off, get us all three shot to pieces!"

They drifted outside, Doc patently unwilling to share their discomposure with the stranger in the dirty boiled shirt with sleeve garters and false teeth that didn't fit.

"Doc, be reasonable, for chrissakes!"

"Me, be reasonable? ME?"

"Don't get mad."

"Me, get mad? ME?"

Raider snatched the paper from his hand and waved it high.

"This here is a ticket to disaster, that's what this is. He not only wants us to ring 'em in but turn the whole works over to 'em, us sit back an' let them carry the goddamn ball. I said it afore, I say it again: The man's a twenty-one carat, four-square asshole! He doesn't know Indians, he doesn't know the West, all he knows is how to squeeze nickels an' dimes outta our expense sheets. How to line our pockets with blood!"

Doc's expression in reaction to this clearly indicated that the clashing of metaphors slightly jarred him.

"*We* got to do this, Doc, us three."

He crumpled the message, dropped it to the ground, and mashed it with his heel.

Doc shook his head. "I don't like it any better than you, but orders are orders. We'll ride out to Fort Gunther and discuss it with the commandant."

"You ride out an' discuss it. I'm headin' back to that camp, an' pronto." He jerked his head and his glance toward Aaron. "You comin'?"

"I . . ."

"He's coming with me," said Doc tightly.

"Good. You two go call on the Army. Walk in on 'em hand in hand. I'm pullin' out."

To Aaron's astonishment, and to that of two well-dressed ladies floating by carrying knitting baskets, Doc reared back and sent his right fist crashing against Raider's jaw, knocking him cold.

"Whooooooo-eeeee," said Aaron hoarsely, his eyes straining at their sockets. "Wha'ja do that fer?"

"Sling him over his saddle. How far to Fort Gunther?"

"Fifty, sixty miles."

"Wonderful."

They tied Raider belly down over his saddle and started out, heading into the badlands, the landscape cluttered with hundreds of hills mostly tan but with bands of red, pink, and brown, with needle-and-thread and blue grama thriving between them. The narrow road curled and twisted. The sun found them and concentrated its fury mercilessly. Raider came to about three miles from town, jounced awake.

"Hey, Doc."

"Yes, Rade?"

"Sorry if my face hurt your knuckles. Where we headin'? As if I didn' know. Hey, these ropes are cuttin' into my wrists an' ankles somethin' fierce, and bent over like this is bustin' my back, my ribs, hipbones. . . . Isn' doin' my kidneys much good."

"Your kidneys aren't in front."

"Mine move aroun'."

Doc pulled up and Aaron did likewise. Together they untied Raider. He rubbed his wrists to restore circulation, twisting his face so painfully as he did so, so melodramatically that Doc laughed and shook his head.

"I did it for your own good," he said.

"Oh hell, I know that. Didn't I kayo you one time for your own good?"

"I don't remember."

Raider swung and knocked him cold. "See if you can remember that."

"Oh, for the love o' Jesus," said Aaron, stunned.

Raider drew on him. "Don' go tryin' anythin' fancy, son."

"I thought you two was friends."

"Close as skin. Give a hand, we'll toss him over his saddle. We're headin' for the Oglalas' camp. You can either come or not. Nobody's gonna force you. It's up to you."

"We're supposed to get help from the Army."

"I know, but we're not. We've blown 'nough time jabberin' an' jerkin' aroun' already. Chrissakes, by the time we get there she'll have gray hair an' a damn cane. What'll it be?"

Aaron shrugged. "You're dealin'."

"We don' have to tie him. I'm not what you call sadistic like him. You ride up front, you'll lead his mount. We'll be headin' northeast."

They reached the Oglalas' camp the evening of the second day. Fifty yards from it Raider could see that Crazy Horse and his men had come back and left again. All that remained were a number of burial scaffolds with corpses atop them snugly wrapped in hides and tied with buffalo sinew. Doc had long since given up arguing over their destination. He had given in completely to Raider after pointedly reminding him that total responsibility for their defiance of agency orders would be his to answer to.

Raider dismounted and poked through a cook fire with the toe of his boot.

"Still warm. They musta pulled out last night or this mornin'."

"Did it look anything like this when you left?"

"I told you. The lodges were still standin', they scaffolded the dead they brought back, an' the women an' children were gone, took away by the Crows."

"Crazy Horse sure 'nough musta caught up with them Crows an' beat them proper," observed Aaron. "Else they wouldn'a got their dead back, ain't that so, Mr. Raider?"

"That's so, Mr. Fales. There's lots more here now than before."

"You don't suppose one of these bodies could be—" began Doc.

"Hell no, she's back with them. She's got to be."

"Got to be. Let's examine them, just to make sure."

Aaron swallowed, paling slightly. "I plumb hate to look at dead folks, 'specially fresh kilt."

"Stay put," said Raider. "We'll keep all the fun to ourselves."

They set about the grisly task. They fashioned makeshift ladders, using lodgepoles, sticks, and sinew, and climbed up to examine the corpses. Raider found He-Dog, neatly scalped and with his throat cut. He was smiling, or was it a grimace? Raider asked himself. Doc, meanwhile had found a body evidently trapped in a burning tepee and charred beyond recognition. It smelled vile, a sickly sweet odor that turned his stomach.

"Rade, come here."

"What?"

"Come and see."

Raider muttered and moved his ladder up alongside Doc's. He climbed up unsteadily. Doc held up a blackened hand. Raider gasped.

"Son of a bitch!"

"What's up?" asked Aaron from below.

"It's a ring," said Doc.

A white crown set in a large ruby surrounded by melted gold. On one side of the crown was the letter H, on the other, an I. The last time Raider had seen it was shortly before mounting his pony and setting out with Crazy Horse and his warriors to attack the Crows.

CHAPTER THIRTEEN

Gently but firmly, Doc pushed away Queen Ernestine's head, releasing his manhood from her soft, wet mouth. She straightened, smiling lecherously. He felt as if by some perverted prank of nature, by some method of malefic magic he had been fileted, every bone in his body removed without a single drop of blood being spilt. But as a result, he could not move his torso; spineless as it was, he had no control over it. The room surrounding the bed was filled with fluffy white clouds, obscuring walls and ceiling and the other furnishings. Ernestine only was visible, bending again, preparing to go back to work on him. He tried to hold her away with one arm, but when he raised it it fell down, coiling in a pile.

He woke, snapping up to a sitting position. Nearby, Aaron lay sleeping contentedly, his lips fluttering lightly at the tail of a snore in the faint glow of moving light. Doc rubbed his eyes, suddenly aware of the source of the light: fire in the sky. Raider was standing at the top of a ladder, torch in hand, bending over Milena's uncovered and blackened corpse. He had taken the precaution of fixing a split section of a branch over his nose to prevent his inhaling the sickening odor. His torch flared eerily, man and fire framed by the starless sky. He looked like some demon ascending from hell in a William Blake painting, reflected Doc, suppressing a mild shudder.

"Rade . . ."

"Ssssh, you'll wake him."

"What are you looking for? We've got the ring. Come down here."

To Doc's surprise, Raider unfastened his nose, pocketed the stick, and descended the ladder without protest. He dropped the torch into the dying embers of the fire on his way over to him.

"You woke me out of a sound sleep."

"I tried to be quiet."

"What are you up to? Why uncover—"

"Something's wrong, Doc."

"What?"

"That's just it, I don' know. It just isn' right. Why would the Crows kill her?"

"Maybe they didn't. Maybe it was the Oglalas. Maybe she was killed accidentally, the lodge she was in set fire . . ."

"She would have got out."

"Maybe she was asleep. Maybe tied hand and foot."

"Why would either of 'em tie her? She was no threat. If they were gonna kill her they would have right off, not hang onto her, dress her, feed her, an' then do it."

"She could have been killed accidentally, as I said, maybe a stray bullet . . ."

"No."

Raider had crouched beside him where he lay. Aaron snored softly. In the glow of the embers Doc could see Raider's profile sharply outlined, as if cut out of copper. He knew that look, the heart-set, stubborn look of resistance to all arguments and opinions contrary to the conviction firmly anchored in the man's mind. It was, mused Doc, useless to speak up, to add to his array of possible practical explanations.

"It's not her."

Doc pursed forth a jet of breath in exasperation. Reaching into his shirt pocket, he took out Allan Pinkerton's telegram. He unwrapped it, disclosing the partially melted ruby ring.

"What's this?"

"I know. It's hers. *But that's not her up there.*"

"Why not? Is it too small, too big? On second thought,

how can you possibly tell? It's burnt to the bone, it could be shrunken to half.''

"You didn't know her like I got to. She was a helluva woman, Doc. Oh sure, horny as a tom cat, but tough, strong-minded, the sort who gets her way come hell or high water, even with Mr. Feathers. Indians respect people with grit. Crazy Horse did her. They treated her like what she was—top o' the ladder.''

"I'll take your word for how tough she was. I only remember her as imperious and arrogant.''

"She was like that in the camp, walkin' roun' with that walk o' hers, shoulders back, nose in the air, that look on her face like she was all the time smellin' a dead fish. She could shrink you in your boots jus' lookin' you up an' down, man, boy, everybody.''

"She could have been Cleopatra, Joan of Arc, that still doesn't make her indestructible. Listen to me. We have to bring the body back with us. It's our duty to. Besides, the king and Ernestine will demand it. They'll want it returned to Montenegro for proper burial. There'll probably be a state funeral. When we bring it in they're certain to want a doctor to examine it, although for the life of me I don't know what he'd be able to determine.''

"I got it! GOT IT!''

Aaron jumped up, reaching for his rifle, shaking out the cobwebs.

"Rade . . .''

"I've figured it out! That's not her, it's not. It's Black Shawl with Milena's ring! She give it to her!''

"That's preposterous. This ring is royal property. She'd never give it to anybody. It would be completely contrary to her code of values, her regal consciousness, if you will.''

"She give it to Black Shawl. They were gettin' close as sisters. She tol' me so herself. What happened was Black Shawl admired it so she jus' whipped it off her finger and handed it over. That's exactly what happened. That's all bullshit, code o' values, regal con . . . whatever the hell. She did like she pleased when she pleased to. That was her only code. Shit, man, you think kidnappin' my ass was part o' any code o' values? Jumpin' in the sheets with a uneducated Fulton County sodbuster, suckin', fuckin', an' carryin' on generally like a mink with a splinter up its ass? You think that showed regal con, con . . ."

"Calm down. Did she ever suggest she might give this to Black Shawl?"

"Didn' I jus' tell you, for chrissakes?"

"What's goin' on, fellers?" asked Aaron thickly.

"Nothin', go back to sleep," snapped Raider.

"No, stay awake," snapped Doc.

"Which?"

"Mr. Raider thinks that burnt corpse is not the queen's. He says it's Crazy Horse's squaw's, that Queen Milena gave this ring to her." Doc paused. He could see nothing in Aaron's eyes, not a glimmer of understanding. Wide open and blank, they stared back at him. He sighed. "It's okay, go back to sleep. Sorry we woke you."

Aaron lay down and was immediately asleep.

Raider snatched the ring from Doc. He tossed it lightly in the air and caught it again. "I just thought o' somethin'."

"Can't any of this wait until morning?"

"Black Shawl had a crease across her neck like a rope burn. Whenever she'd lift her head you could see it plain as day." He rescued the torch from the fire, tossed the ring back to Doc, and, returning to the scaffold, climbed the ladder.

"Well?"

"I can't tell. It's all just black black bone, not a lick o' flesh." He descended the ladder, coming back to where Doc lay. "But I'm still right. I know I am. She's still with him. Like the boy said, he musta licked the Crows. How else could he get back his dead? He got the women and children back too, and her." He turned his head, studying the horizon to the north. "They're out there somewheres, and she's with him. Tomorrow we start lookin'."

CHAPTER FOURTEEN

Doc privately disagreed with his partner's contention that Black Shawl's remains reposed atop the funeral scaffold and not Queen Milena's. On two counts, he disagreed: The ring was a symbol of the ruling house of Montenegro, not a piece of personal adornment. Technically, it was not Milena's property to give, and she knew it. Secondly, that she may have been accidentally killed was a possibility verging on the probable, at least in Doc's mind. Helpless, unarmed civilians caught between two opposing forces were all too often victims.

For his part, Raider searched for and found additional arguments to buttress his stand. He pointed out that Crazy Horse would never accord a white captive, man or woman, the Oglalas' sacred funeral rites, the scaffold or fork of a tree, the ceremonial wrappings, and the feet placed toward the east. After decomposition, bodies were sometimes taken down and deposited in rock crevices. The scaffolds would eventually rot and collapse, at which time, a couple of years hence, more or less, the Oglalas would return to bury the remains and mark the graves with piles of stones.

But more compelling than any fact or assumption Raider could propound was Doc's own long-standing faith in his partner's instincts. And Raider would never stick by his guns out of pure obstinacy unless his bones assured him that he was right. He was too honorable a soul to ride unshod over another's viewpoint purely for the satisfaction of appearing right.

Raider continued dead set against Allan Pinkerton's order to alert the nearest Army camp or fort and enlist the commandant's aid.

"Don't go givin' me rules an' regulations an' orders from the agency, Doc," he said airily as they mounted and prepared to leave the next morning. "You bend 'em to suit you jus' as much as I do."

"I certainly do not, and I resent your saying so!"

"Oh, yeah? What 'bout those two Secret Service fellas back there in Kansas City? You said yourself the chief ordered you to cooperate with 'em, work han' in glove. Shit! Practically the minute you got hold o' Tucker's telegram you ran outta there like a cat with its tail afire. You couldn' shake those two fast 'nough."

"That was different."

"How so?"

"I had every intention of contacting them as soon as something concrete in the way of clues materialized."

"You never did."

"There wasn't time. I didn't even take time to eat or sleep, hardly."

"All he could think 'bout was findin' you two, an' quick as he could," chimed in Aaron.

Raider grunted. "What you tryin' to do, Mr. Fales, make me feel guilty?"

"Yup."

Doc snickered, then sobered. "Where do we head, Rade? Any ideas, or do we just ride around until we drop from our saddles from old age?"

"We follow our trail, what the hell you think we do." He took a last look around. The fire was out and scattered, Black Shawl's body carefully rewrapped, the ladders broken, the pieces scattered, and all other evidence of their visit disposed of. "Let's go."

Allan Pinkerton sat back in his chair in his fancy, brown-striped, white-ground Penang Laundered shirt-sleeves, stretching his solid brown elastic web suspenders with his thumbs.

He was boiling mad, and addressed his office manager between clenched teeth in a voice that reasonably compared with that of a disgruntled mountain lion. He did not frighten Edward Wagner, however. His manager had seen his superior in such a mood so often, heard his threats and vilification and seen him on the verge of exploding into little pieces of flesh and bone so many times, the performance had become a bore.

"Ooperatives Weatherbee and Raider hov seen fit to totally disregard explicit orders from their coomonder-ond-chief. Their conduct is ootragious ond obomonoble. The two of them are well oware, ocutely oware that President Gront is stonding over me with the sword of Domocles in hond like the Ongel of Death prepared to strike ot ony moment. Tis nae bod enoof the two of thom hov misplaced the woman. Even worse, she may ot this very moment be as dead as Kelsey's cow, or failing thot is destined to be rescued not by oos, duly ossigned ond ongaged to protect the lot, boot by the Army, the Navy, the Secret Service, ony bodge or roscally nosy-Hogan who sees fit to onject himself into this wretched offair. Which leaves only one thing for it."

"What's that?"

"Oxtraordinory measures, what else? Alert Robert in Denver. Onstrooct him to ossign every, thot is, every mon ot his disposal to trock doon Raider and Weatherbee, find them, haul them in, divest them of their authority, coonfiscate their I.D. cards, ond turn thom over to the law oon a charge of oobstruction of joostice, reckloss ondangorment of the life ond limb of a foreign dignatory whose person is oonder the protection of the United States goovernment, disobeying a presidential order, ontentionol ond deliborate failure to cooperate with the Secret Service, blatant—"

Up shot Wagner's hands, stopping him. "Do we really want to resort to such extremes, I mean bring in our own operatives? The agency'll look a laughingstock."

"Ond what does it look noo, may I be so bold os to onquire? We couldn't look more foolish to the scondolmongering press thon if we ossembled ourselves in Union Square ond proceeded to run aroond in the oltogether tossing roses ot each other. Do os you're told, mon. Get word off to Robert!''

"You're making a mistake.''

"DOMNED IF I OM! DOMNED IF I'LL SIT HERE LISTENING TO ONY MORE OF YOUR LIP!''

"All right, all right, all right.''

"Thot's better.''

Pinkerton paused, cleared his throat, and lowered his eyes and the fire therein. "I dinna mean to raise my voice. The foct is I feel ot my wit's ond. Ond it's those two who've put me there. Ploocking thom oot of the game is noo the first order of the day. Once we're rid of thom I dinna care who rescues the woman. Letting someone else do it con scarcely ottroct ony more humiliation ond omborrossmont thon we already hov, thonks to Raider ond noo Weatherbee.''

"What if they find her before Robert and his men can?''

"In thot oonlikely event it will go no easier for thom, on thot point I con ossure you.'' Picking up his ruler, he snapped it in half. "I would give six years off my life ond ten thoosand dollars in gold to hov the twa of thom here in this office at this very moment. What is the penalty for premeditated murder in the state of Illinois? Honging, it moost be. I'd donce oop the gollow's steps with a song on my lips. Go, get to it, mon.''

Wagner hesitated, clearing his throat.

"What is it?''

"There's a bunch of newspaper reporters in the waiting room.''

"Is there noo?''

Straightening in his chair, Pinkerton's hand shot to the handle of the lower drawer of his desk. He jerked it open and brought out a Navy Colt. Wagner skirted the desk and seized him by the wrist.

"Calm down! Calm down, for heaven's sakes.''

"Dinna be doft. I wasn't aboot to shoot the scondolmongering vermin. I merely wanted to frighten thom oot the door. This isn't even loaded. It won't be oontil Raider ond Weatherbee are on their way bock.''

• • •

Raider, Doc, and Aaron followed the trail for the next several days, losing it, picking up what Raider thought it was, losing it again and a third time. They questioned everyone they passed, including a small hunting party of Blackfeet passing through the badlands, climbing into the Bighorn Mountains. They camped by a stream one night in a heavy downpour. Doc was discouraged, and made no effort to hide it. He could put up with the discomforts and shortcomings of the trail for only so long. Beyond that point, fixed firmly, immovably by his nature in place, his tolerance deserted him. The seat of his trousers no longer stuck to him, nor did his cheeks or his back ache from the long hours in the saddle. It was all the little things taken in combination that roused and raised his resentment.

"A drink of decent whiskey, a comfortable bed with a feather pillow, two feather pillows, a properly aged and cooked steak, ice cream. Do you know that I haven't tasted ice cream in, what is it, more than a year?"

"My heart's bleedin' so I just may douse the fire," said Raider dryly, adjusting the buffalo hide lean-to over the little cook fire and removing the coffeepot. "Coffee, anybody?"

"No, thank you," responded Doc.

Aaron eagerly accepted a cup. Doc sat with his knees up, his derby tilted forward, rain collecting around the brim; when he occasionally and thoughtlessly bent forward, it spilled down his front. He was grumbling incoherently.

"Wha'ja say?" asked Raider.

"This is ridiculous."

"The coffee or the rain?"

"You're hilarious. I'm talking about this whole fiasco, and that's the only word for it. We'll never find her. We don't even know if she's still alive, if any of them are."

"I thought we decided she was."

"You decided," Doc snapped. "Neither of us had any say in the matter. I'm past caring whether she is or not."

"That's not a very nice thing to say. Sure you don' want some coffee? Warm you up."

"No, thank you!" Doc seethed briefly before launching on a different tack. "You both realize we've botched this thing from pillar to post."

"How's that, Doc?" asked Aaron innocently.

"Our instructions were to maintain contact with the chief and Harrigan and Gillespie. We were given explicit orders. We blissfully ignored them and continue to do so. Hasn't it occurred to you, Raider, that if we'd done as we were told, regardless of what happens we wouldn't have to shoulder responsibility for the consequences all by ourselves?"

"Fuck the responsibility."

"Oh yes, by all means. Play it exactly as you please, by ear."

"By brain, Doc. Common sense. Horse sense."

"Oh, shut up!"

Aaron was looking from one to the other, back and forth, back and forth. Doc shot him a glare.

"Don't do it, Aaron."

"What, Doc?"

"Don't ask if we're friends. You keep asking, we keep telling you."

Aaron round-eyed him. "That's magic! How'd you know I was goin' to ask? You're a regular mind reader!"

"Oh, shut up!"

Aaron looked properly hurt. The corners of his eyes sagged and his lower lip pushed against his upper, bowing his mouth, crinkling his brow. He and Raider sipped in silence. Doc shivered and drew himself tighter into himself.

"This rain's a blessing," he murmured. "It's sure to wipe out every trace of their trail. We'll have no choice but to go back."

"Where? Kansas City?" asked Raider.

"Back to civilization. Do you two realize we haven't seen a white man in three days?"

"What you got against Mr. Feathers?"

"It's not what I've got against him, it's the other way around. Look, I've gone along with you this far against my better judgment. It's been your way all the way. Let me talk—I'm entitled to that much. It's been your hunches and gut feelings, your inspired guesswork every step since you crawled into our camp looking like Desert Pete, the prospector, and smelling like his burro.''

Aaron tittered. Doc ignored him.

"But all good things have to come to an end. I've reached mine. You two can go on if you want to. I'm going back.''

"You can't, Doc. We're a team. You can't break up the team.''

"I can and I intend to. I didn't sign on to ride blindfolded into the pit with you or anybody else blindfolded leading the way. I'm going back and hand in my resignation. This assignment, the job itself, has become more than flesh and blood can stand. As of now, gentlemen, I quit!''

Raider's reaction to this was to look around him a full 360 degrees. Doc watched him, his forehead twisting questioningly.

Raider explained. "Just lookin' round for somebody for you to quit to.''

"Try Allan Pinkerton. First thing tomorrow I'm heading for the nearest railroad and a free ride back to Chicago. On second thought, Denver is closer. I can hand over my I.D. card and code book to Robert.''

"You will hang round for breakfast. You'll want to. We'll be havin' coffee.''

"I mean what I say, Rade.''

"He purely does, Mr. Raider.''

"Shit, Mr. Fales! He's beat, he's achin', he's wet, he's down, an' he doesn' much like my coffee, but tomorrow the sun'll come up, an' he'll have a good night's rest an' sweet dreams tucked snug under his outta-sortsness. The whole world'll look diff'rent.''

"Don't bet on it,'' muttered Doc, and scoffed with venomous disdain. "Out-of-sortsness. Incredible! I've never met anybody who butchers the King's English like you. Frailty, thy name is woman; illiteracy, thy name is Raider!''

Whatever his name in his partner's eyes, Raider's prophecy proved to be on target. In the morning Doc made no mention of leaving or resigning. The sun came up full, fat, and pure gold. It drenched the sodden landscape, drying out everything it touched, setting the mica and quartz in the rocks glistening, brightening the conifers' varying shades of green, and causing the stream, splashing merrily from stone to stone to sparkle so it resembled an undulating mass of diamonds. Through the trees below to the northwest they could see Wandering Creek creeping around the rocks. Beyond it . . .

"Visitors," murmured Raider ominously.

A file of Indians—a hunting party from their dress, the absence of war bonnets and war paint, the antelope carcasses stripped and cleaned, riding their ponies' withers. The last two in the line pulled travois loaded with buffalo carcasses wrapped in hides.

Raider snapped his fingers. "Mr. Fales, get the horses back behind that big rock an' keep 'em quiet. Move."

Aaron gathered the reins and fled, picking his way nimbly through the rocks. Raider and Doc lay prone, staring down at the passers-by.

"What tribe are they, Rade?"

"Search me. This is Sioux country, Oglalas country."

"Are they Crazy Horse's?"

"I can't tell. I'm no expert on Mr. Feathers."

"Don't you recognize any?"

"I'm lookin'."

"This could be the break we need. If they are with Crazy Horse they could lead us straight to her. They're obviously done with their hunting and heading back to camp."

Aaron came back, flattening beside Doc.

"I don' reco'nize a one," said Raider dejectedly. "Still, they was so many."

Doc bit his lip and frowned. "We can't let them just saunter on by."

"How 'bout we ask 'em up for coffee?"

"Shut up!"

"Ssssh, for chrissakes!"

"Aaron," rasped Doc, "get the horses. We'll follow them. You ride to the nearest post and get help."

''That'll be Fort Edgerton,'' said Raider. ''Sixty, seventy mile east. An' where does he come back to when he does get help? Who's to know where we're gonna end up?''

Doc indicated Wandering Creek below. ''Where the creek bends around that huge rock. One of us'll ride back and meet you there.''

''When?'' asked Aaron.

''Sunup tomorrow,'' said Raider. ''One o' us . . . Son of a bitch, I don' believe it, I purely don'!''

His jaw had sagged in amazement. His eyes bulged, his pointing finger waggled. Bringing up the rear of the line, with loaded travois tied to their ponies, were two huge braves. Their skin was unusually pale—even lighter than Crazy Horse's. They were naked to the waist, their pink chests gleaming in the glare of the sun like burnished shields. They had on buckskin trousers and moccasins. Both carried bows, their quivers slung on their backs.

''They're white men,'' murmured Doc.

''Whiter'n I'll ever be,'' said Raider.

Aaron gawked. ''It's them, Mr. Raider. Her two body-guards.''

Raider was nodding slowly. ''Karel an' Bela.''

CHAPTER FIFTEEN

The shadows of clouds darkened the valley, with patches of sunlight between gleaming in contrast. To the east the Green Bottom River, its clear, cool waters nurtured by winter snows and springs, eased languidly through the land. High bluffs rose at the bends of the river, overgrown with rose vines wearing myriad delicate pink blossoms. At the distant end of the valley in the slate-colored hills a lone bighorn appeared, ambling down from the rim, his headdress, at once preposterous and magnificent, framing his slender, white-muzzled face. A brace of red-tailed hawks glided by overhead, and in the timber lining the river, Western tanagers, horned larks, and brown creepers sang unseen.

Here and there in the valley blue flowers betrayed the hiding places of prairie turnip roots to digging squaws. Other blossoms abounded, betraying by their presences nothing but their beautiful and varied colors: blue columbine, whose nectar-filled spurs attracted hummingbirds; delicate blue and white lupines; slender pink elephant head; and Indian paintbrush splashing the view with vivid crimson.

Established in this tranquil scene were the camp circles, six gatherings of Sioux and one of Cheyenne, extending nearly a mile along the line of the river. Among their lodges, from the perspective of the passing hawks, were countless brush and willow wickiups, homes to nationless warriors who had allied themselves with the two tribes.

The camp was enormous, much too large to continue so assembled for many days. The hordes of ponies would speedily consume all the available grasses. In the camp circle of the Oglalas most of the ponies had been collected and hobbled by the youngsters. Crazy Horse's favorite war-horse, a sturdy-legged yellow pinto blanketed and tied to a tree, swished its tail, sending a green fly buzzing off.

In his lodge Crazy Horse sat alone on a buffalo robe, his war bundle before him. The sight of it purported to rekindle his courage. Each article in the bundle was a symbol of bravery: a human scalp with braided hair, recent property of Seven Knives and not yet thoroughly dried; an eagle's claw; a hawk's bone whistle; a collection of thirteen herbs bound in the pelt of a hare. He wore his breechclout and his "ghost shirt" of buckskin sewn with sinew, the arms hung with feathers, the front, above and below, with slender braids of human hair, and decorated with symbols revealed to the wearer in his visions. His shirt, his unopened war bundle before him, and his taboos uppermost in mind (never pick up anything found, never point at anything except with his thumb, never touch metal to his lips, never neglect to cleanse his body and his weapons twice daily), these rigid dictates and others governed his conduct as the titular head of his people.

But as he sat cross-legged in the semidarkness, contemplating his war bundle, thoughts of taboos, responsibilities, and the great task facing him were dislodged from his mind by the memory of Black Shawl. His wife had been a good woman, and he had loved her, doted upon her in unchiefly ways in the eyes of enemies and friends alike, parading the equality of their relationship for all to see, as he exhibited his unpainted body, save in battle: no paint, no feathers, few ornaments, disdaining such trifles, such ostentation.

He thought of Black Shawl: her shyness, her lovely, limpid eyes so like a timid doe's, her skin as flawless as a child's, her slender girl's body, and the way she walked, so lightly, floating from step to step. He pictured the rope burn on her neck where her drunken father had lassoed her as she ran from him to escape his lust. She had fought and freed herself, keeping herself pure for her husband. He thought of her wracking cough that raised the veins in her neck and in her forehead and brought tears to her eyes, but never a complaint to her lips. Years before, she had borne him a daughter in great pain. The child had lived to the fourth snows, dancing, laughing, jabbering like the black-billed magpie. She had caught the whooping cough. Blue Wolf, the shaman, had tried to drive the evil from her lungs but failed. Together, he and Black Shawl with He-Dog had taken the child to a white doctor in a settlement near Bright Stove cave, but too late. As he was preparing to examine her she died. Black Shawl had been grief-stricken, as had he. Their bereavement drew them even closer. Now Black Shawl herself was dead, burned to death in the lodge.

So many were dead: He-Dog, Blue Wolf, Conquering Bear, Man Afraid, White Wolf—so many braves with hearts so huge, so filled with courage they stretched the cages of their ribs. And Red Cloud was dying, and others would die, soon. . . .

A wedge of sunlight angled down upon the war bundle. Crazy Horse lifted his eyes. It was Milena, who had taken the name Towana, Whiter-Skin-Than-Mine, his wife. Woman's arms and thighs and mouth replacing Black Shawl. Not replacing; no one could ever take her place. But Towana was good, as she had been good, though perhaps too much in awe of him. Black Shawl for all her shyness had never been in awe of him, of anyone, even Red Cloud. But Towana was a good wife, quick to learn, understand, and accept the ways of the Oglalas. Willing, eager to belong.

She too wore a "ghost shirt," the same in appearance as his own, but without the vision markings. She had yet to see her first vision. He did not encourage it. When a warrior saw visions and recounted them to his brothers, if they impressed them they lent the visionary new stature and respect. In time such men became leaders, even chiefs. Women did not. Why then should they strive to see visions? They could not become chiefs among the Oglalas, only among the dung eaters. Red Cloud had told them in council of Woman Chief, who could

ride, shoot, and hunt with any warrior. The Crows had
kidnapped her from her people, the Gros Ventre, when she
was a child, and she had grown up with them. She had killed
her first enemy, a Blackfoot, wounded two others, and sent
two more fleeing. From then on she was called Woman Chief
and was permitted to sit in Crow war councils. She led many
raids and defended Crow lands, even against her own people.
She reputedly had many coups until she was killed by her
own people, the Gros Ventre.

He nodded and Towana entered, kneeling across from him,
then pushing her slender legs out to one side in the prescribed
manner. She did not speak, nor did he.

He had tried for nis first vision when a mere boy, long
before he took his father's name, when all in the tribe called
him Curly. He had been with his father and mother in a Brulé
camp. It was a time of trouble, and his mother wanted to be
with her own people. It had been a bountiful fall in the
country of the Running Water, the currant bushes heavy with
their sweet berries, the wild plums turning yellow and becoming edible, so juicy just the thought of them made his mouth
water. The antelope ran, the quail and curlew and ducks
abounded, easy game for a boy of twelve.

By chance he had been present when Conquering Bear was
shot and wounded by the soldiers. He had seen him die in his
lodge, seen his eyes close and the life rattle out of his
throat—its farewell to his shrunken body. He had run from
the lodge to be by himself away on the bluffs, to think over
what he had seen, the reasons for it, the lack of reasons, the
white man and his hatred, his guns and cannons.

He had hobbled his pony and, placing the sharpest stones
he could find between his toes and piling pebbles under his
spine to keep him awake, lay down on a flat rock, all day, all
night, and the next day as well. No creature came near him,
not even a gnat rising from the river below. He saw no birds.
He could not hear the breeze sigh, for he was by now too
deep inside himself, ignoring the burning of his eyes, his
swollen, aching limbs and back.

A second night, a third day he stayed flat on the rock,

struggling to steal a vision from his fevered imagination, but none presented itself. It was almost dark at the third day's end when his father came, shaking him, breaking into the limbo filling his mind, angry, impatient with him, jerking him to his feet. He explained that he had come to this place alone to await a vision. And his father had laughed and ridiculed him, for he had not even bothered to make his preparations. He had not fasted; he had left without consulting with his holy man father, with Blue Wolf, or anyone, without even telling anyone where he was going. He was twelve. His visions were patient; they would wait for him. They had.

He pointed to Towana with his thumb. Permission granted, she spoke.

"When will you leave?"

"We wait for Iron Hawk and the Hunkpapas and more Sans Arcs. We must make preparations: the sacrifice of the scarlet blanket, the Sun Dance."

"But the grass will all be eaten in only a few days."

"Then our ponies will not eat until after the battle is won."

"The first hunters have returned. They have brought much meat. They are the group my men were with. They did well with your weapons."

"They are strong. Strong arm, sharp eye, good bow. Sit here beside me." She hesitated to move. "You are still afraid of me."

"I am afraid of no one."

"Your eyes argue with your words. Come to me, wife, prepare your body."

Raider and Doc followed the hunting party all morning long. The Indians moved at a leisurely pace. They appeared relaxed, laughing and joking, one goading and teasing another, setting the rest laughing. Bela and Karel were studiously ignored. Neither seemed to mind.

"They're jus' like dogs, Doc. She could stand 'em in corners an' they'd stay there without a word or whimper till they collapsed from hunger. She once told me they'd both kill for her. I believed her."

"Royalty has a stranglehold on their type of mentality, Rade. They're heading into the hills. We'll be able to get closer."

"No hurry."

"How far do you think we've come?"

"No more'n ten or twelve mile. They're movin' slow as molasses."

The hunters climbed into the hills, slipped through a narrow pass, and were lost from view. Raider heeled the sorrel forward. Doc followed in his dust. They reached the top, pulled up, and dismounted. Concealing themselves behind a convenient rock, they peered out each side.

Raider whistled softly. "Sweet Jesus, they mus' be every Indian in the northern territories camped down there, leastwise all the Sioux, I bet: Oglalas, Miniconjous, Brulés, Two Kettles, Sans Arcs, Hunkpapas, Blackfeet . . ."

"Blackfeet?"

"Blackfeet Sioux, not Montana Blackfeet. There's Cheyenne, too. See those warrior robes laid out in the sun, with the red beadin' an' the ridin' figures painted on the top? And that red bullhide shield is Cheyenne. Oh boy, this is Mr. Feathers' Sunday-go-to-meetin' for fair!"

"Shhhh. What are they up to, do you think? Are they going after the whole Crow nation?"

"Not on your tintype, not with this crowd. My guess is they're goin' after the U.S. of A. Doc, there's got to be two thousan' tepees down there. They're thicker'n fleas on a dirty dog!"

The nearest lodges stood less than a hundred and fifty feet away. Doc cast a worried glance behind where they lay. There was nothing but down the hill and open country beyond, all the way back to the hills where they had parted company with Aaron. In his mind Doc pictured the boy dusting along at a good clip. He should be halfway to Fort Edgerton by now. He should arrive by mid-afternoon.

"Rade . . ."

"Yeah?"

"Sunup is much too long. One of us should go back at sundown. Aaron'll be back with the Army by early evening."

"I doubt it. Oh, he'll get there quick 'nough, but you know the Army. Whoever's in charge'll want to contact division headquarters at Fort Leavenworth an' they'll maybe want to contact the chief in Chicago. Maybe the War Department. Whoever's comin' from Edgerton may not get his marchin' orders cut an' okayed 'fore midnight. Figure they'll send out a mounted battalion. They'll move along like snails. An' when they do get here they'll jus' have to turn round an' send back for more bodies. Even if they show up with a regiment, that's only seven hundred. There's got to be three, maybe four thousan' Indians down there." He grinned. "Countin' Karel an' Bela, that is."

"I'm glad you find it amusing."

"What I find it is is fuckin' ridiculous, if you wanta get technical. Anythin' gets as bad as this mess passes the point o' serious an' becomes automatic ridiculous. That's a law o' nature, for chrissakes. Doc, look at the size o' that camp. Seven hundred men surround it they'd be a hundred feet apart. What we oughta do is get to the nearest telegraph key, get in touch with the U.S. White House in Washington, an' get old Unconditional Surrender to send out the Army, Navy, Marines, an' the Texas Rangers!"

"If it's any consolation, at least we're starting to do things right. We're obeying orders."

"Oh, do tell!"

Raider's expression was as scornful as he could make it, but even as he displayed it it softened, darkened, became perplexed.

"What's the matter?"

"I'm thinkin' ahead. However many men Fort Edgerton sends over, we can't go bustin' in there after her. There's no call to. They're fixin' to go on the warpath. They're sure not sittin' there waitin' for the Army to jump 'em. They'd be sittin' ducks in this valley, an' they know it. They'll leave their families behind with a guard to protect 'em jus' like the Oglalas did when they lit out after the Crows.

"That's when we grab her."

• • •

The time had arrived for Crazy Horse to sacrifice the scarlet blanket and to arrange for the Sun Dance. Selecting eight warriors representing the eight different tribes, he sent them forth to select a symbolic Enemy. They decided upon a small cottonwood tree. The entire encampment assembled around it and watched as the eight warriors struck it with their coupsticks. Then a group of six chaste and highly respected squaws felled the tree. Its branches were trimmed, and they carried it back to Crazy Horse's tepee, bearing it on poles, since contact with the Enemy was forbidden to anyone except the holy men who presided over the ritual and those who had previously danced the Sun Dance.

A hole was dug and the tree stood upright in it. It was painted red on the west side, blue on the north, green on the east, and yellow on the south. Bound to its top were a red robe, offerings of tobacco and cherrywood sticks, and two pieces of dried buffalo hide, one cut in the shape of a buffalo, the other in the shape of a man. While these preparations were carried out, the holy men met in privacy and prayed for clear skies and a bright sun.

Crazy Horse was acutely aware that only repeated demonstrations of unflinching courage would secure his prestige and the continuing respect of his people. He was mindful as well that the debacle involving the dung eaters had cast a shadow over his reputation, despite the fact that Seven Knives' scalp now reposed in his war bundle. Victory in the battle to come would reinforce his claim to leadership. But first must come the sacrifice of the scarlet blanket.

The holy men returned and ceremoniously painted his hands and feet red. Across his shoulders they painted blue stripes in token of the sky. He sat on the ground, his legs straight before him, his back firmly against the trunk of the sacred tree. Silence fell over the onlookers, so heavy that the only audible sound was that of the breeze deserting the river and rustling the leaves of the trees crowding the near bank.

Crazy Horse began to pray, a singsong plea to the Great Spirit. Lame Elk, who since the death of He-Dog had become his closest brother-friend, acted as his assistant. Holding an awl and a sharp knife, he knelt beside his praying chief. He drew blood from Crazy Horse's right wrist: He pierced the skin with the awl and, lifting a pea-sized piece of tissue, sliced it free with the knife. Blood spurted forth. Awl and knife moved dexterously up the arm, piercing, lifting, cutting—fifty tiny chunks from wrist to shoulder in five neatly aligned rows of ten excisions each.

Crazy Horse did not flinch, did not permit his eyes to blink. The only evidence that excruciating pain was taking possession of him was the appearance of tiny beads of sweat on his brow and across the depression separating his chin from his lower lip. On he chanted as Lame Elk shifted his awl and knife to his left arm to repeat the scarification. Soon both arms were crimson with blood. It slid down to the tips of his fingers, dark droplets plopping silently into the dust.

The scarlet blanket.

Milena stood silently looking on. Even before the first piercing and cutting of tissue, seeing Lame Elk's tools, anticipating what was to come, her hand went to her mouth to stifle protest and she shrank back trembling. Fascinated, mesmerized, she watched the ceremony without a murmur, without moving other than to lower her hand from her mouth.

Gradually, the scarlet blanket congealed. Now Crazy Horse rose from the sacred trunk and, standing upright, turned to face the sun. He began bobbing up and down on his toes, lightly, almost effortlessly, for he would continue to do so all day and must conserve his strength. As he danced he continued to pray, his eyes fixed on the sun as it climbed to its zenith, occasionally lowering his gaze to its lower rim to keep from blinding himself.

On he danced and stared, with no food or water all day. The sun ascended to the top of the sky, hung there briefly, and started down. Hours passed. The sun reached the rim of the hills and slowly sank beneath it. The gray of evening nestled in the valley. On he danced without stopping, all night, driving himself to complete exhaustion. Just before noon the next day he became dizzy. He swayed, staggered, and collapsed, dying a passing death.

Very slowly consciousness returned. The blackness that clouded his mind dissolved and a vision appeared, a scene of battle, blue soldiers in disarray on the side of a hill. They were surrounded and being cut down, their corpses scattered about, the dying covered with blood. The guidon fell and the flag. The bugler blowing retreat took an arrow full in the chest and fell dead, his bugle slipping from his hands. The slender stream idling by the foot of the hill ran red with blood. The air was filled with blue smoke, arrows came whirring in from all sides, and lances, skillfully hurled, struck one man after another.

The scene vanished. Crazy Horse opened his eyes and smiled.

Raider came riding back from the rendezvous point at four in the morning with Aaron, a Major Howard Delaplane, and ninety fully armed cavalry. The moon was almost full and the stars twinkled in abundance, affording a clear view of the valley below. Delaplane studied the encampment through his binoculars. Cook fires glowed and a few Indians could be seen moving about, but the vast majority slept. From his vantage point, the major could not see Crazy Horse dancing and praying.

Major Delaplane was short and stocky, a pompous, arrogant gamecock, lacking only feathers and claws. The beak he had was as prominent and sharp as the telegraph operator's in the Western Union office in Lemington. His fondest wish, as brazenly evident as his nose, was to take charge. With a vengeance.

"As soon as my reinforcements get here, we'll form up and march in. Confront the red rascals face to face. No shilly-shallying, no mincing words. Demand they hand her over or we'll cut them down."

"Hold it," rasped Raider. "What in hell are you talkin' 'bout man?"

Back snapped the major, "Weren't you listening, soldier?"

"I was, and don' you call me soldier. I'm mufti, an' don't you forget it!"

"Rade . . ." began Doc. "Major Delaplane, with all due respect, I don't think marching in is a good idea. There must be four thousand Indians down there. Now, in a few hours they're going to be moving out in strength. I really think we should hold off."

"Poppycock. Let's get one thing straight: There'll be no shilly-shallying, no pussyfooting and biding our time while I'm in charge here. Every moment's precious. Every moment brings Her Highness that much closer to Azrael. Her life is my responsibility."

"It's ours, too, goddamn it!" burst out Raider. "You go blunderin' in there with ninety men, nine hundred, they'll tear you to fuckin' pieces, an' likely slit her throat! We've nursed this goddamn thing this far without harmin' a hair on her head. I'll be goddamned if we'll let you botch it up now!"

"Now, just a minute, soldier."

"You just a fuckin' minute, Shorty! Our asses are on the line here."

"Rade, shut up!" exclaimed Doc.

"You shut up!"

"You both shut up. Want to rouse the whole camp?" Delaplane glared at Raider, then switched his eyes to Doc. His gaze softened perceptibly. "Let me try to explain, Heatherton."

"His name's Weatherbee!" exclaimed Raider.

The major dismissed him with a wave of one fat arm.

"I know my Indians. You don't have to tell me they're leaving. I know they are. What you have to understand is that sitting there like they are now they don't pose a threat. On the warpath they do. They could raise holy hell. We don't know where they're heading, what they're planning, but we're here in force. Will be in a few hours. We can nip this in the bud. Before they set foot out of there. We surround them—"

"You can," interposed Doc agreeably. "You can attack and possibly cut down half of them. You can kill women and children. You can kill the queen. She happens to be dressed like a squaw, so there's no way you can pick her out of the crowd. If she is killed, you're going to have to answer for it. And my partner and Mr. Fales here and I are going to have to testify at the inquiry. We're going to have to tell the truth."

"In spades," commented Raider, clearing his throat and spitting between the major's feet.

Aaron nodded firmly.

"Your silver leaf can wait, soldier boy. None o' us is gonna catch it, or the lady, your boys or Mr. Feathers, just so you can ride back a fuckin' hero, savvy?"

Delaplane again ignored him. He took Doc by the arm and steered him off to one side. He lowered his voice and spoke pleasantly but firmly.

"I'm in command here, Mr. . . ."

"Weatherbee."

"Weatherbee, Colonel Houston checked with your superiors and the War Department."

"Let's get something straight," said Doc evenly. "We're not questioning your authority. Only your judgment. Think about it: Once Crazy Horse and the rest of the chiefs and the warriors have cleared out you'll be able to walk into that camp like U.S. Grant walked into Appomatox Courthouse."

"No. If I were to permit those savages to ride out I'd be abrogating my responsibility. I can stop them, nip—"

"That's the whole point, Howard: You can't. You don't have the manpower. You don't have the firepower. You could bring every man over from Edgerton and you'd still be outnumbered four or five to one. They're armed to the teeth. It'd be a bloodbath. Now, you were given explicit orders. Your orders are to recover Her Highness and bring her back to your post."

"You're not a military man, Heatherton. I can't expect you to appreciate what we career people call 'military initiative': the ability, the responsibility to take stock of a given situation and take the action appropriate. Even if it requires us to ditch the original plan. Initiative. I personally think adaptability's a better word. Now, get this through your head once and for all, soldier. When the reinforcements get here we're going in.

You three are welcome to come in with us or stay back. That's for you to decide. I intend to attack. Is that clear?''

Doc nodded, smiled, and shook his head.

Bela and Karel, both naked except for breechclouts, sat before Crazy Horse in his lodge. In attendance also were Lame Elk, Red Cloud, Gall, No Neck, and other Sioux chiefs. Bravery was the quality that the Sioux, like their allies, the Cheyenne, most prized and respected. In their leaders, in their warriors.

The two Montenegrins had just finished undergoing the test of courage and endurance which Crazy Horse had subjected himself to earlier. Both men's arms wore the scarlet blanket. So excruciating was his agony, Bela was shaking all over, his teeth tightly clenched as he fought back the urge to scream. Karel was withstanding his pain better, less obviously, but no less uncomfortably. So intense was his pain it seemed to dart to every corner of his body. His arms felt as if he were holding them over a blazing fire, and he could picture gobs of seared flesh dropping from them into the flame.

Now the two initiates were to be confronted with the test of fire. Lame Elk, who had earlier taken the hundred bits of tissue from them, had prepared for this phase by burning a number of little cone-shaped blocks of pith taken from the stalks of sunflowers. The blocks were about half an inch long and resembled the punk used to light firecrackers. Their substance was such as to be able to contain fire for many minutes. Lame Elk placed four of the little blocks on each of their wrists and lit them. The fire quickly began consuming the raw flesh. Karel choked deep in his throat, and the vein lacing the center of his forehead bulged, threatening to rip its casing of flesh, quickly becoming as blue and bruised-looking as the underbelly of a rain cloud. Bela's eyes bulged from their sockets, the tiny veins stretching with blood. Sweat coursed down his face, dripped onto one outstretched arm as he turned his head, and altered the scarlet blanket to pink where it struck.

The test dragged on. Both men's wrists trembled visibly,

but the slowly burning piths did not fall from their wrists. So tightly did they squeeze their fists, their fingernails drew blood from their palms. When the fires finally burned out they were helped to their feet and led away to the sweat bath. Inside the dome-shaped hut the stones were so many and raised to such a high temperature, and the steam was so hot it felt as if their skin were searing. They were given pungent-tasting sage to chew, and they spit on those parts of their flesh that felt as if they had caught fire.

And so they were soothed, cleansed, and gradually restored. And accepted into the Oglalas of Crazy Horse, having proven to his satisfaction that they were capable of enduring any ordeal of the flesh unflinchingly. Karel was given the name Ka-neh-ha-ona, Bull Buffalo Heart, and Bela was called Ka-neh-ha-dowa, Bull Buffalo Horn.

Tonawa was proud. She told them so, and gave each one a gift, a necklace of otter fur which she herself had fashioned.

When the ceremony was completed, Crazy Horse summoned the chiefs of the other tribes and Red Cloud and gave the order to prepare to move out. Within minutes the valley was a scene of utter confusion as the warriors readied themselves, their weapons, and their ponies for combat. Squaws painted their husbands; braves painted each other. From the concealment of rocks overlooking the valley, Raider, Doc and Major Delaplane continued watching. The major became increasingly restless and impatient as the day wore on and the reinforcements from Fort Edgerton failed to appear. He continually checked both his pistols, and when he was not inspecting the chambers and barrels he would whip out a silk handkerchief and polish the barrels and grips vigorously.

His patience finally deserted him altogether, and, summoning a platoon leader, he sputtered orders to dispatch two men to ride back, find the column, and hurry it along.

CHAPTER SIXTEEN

Neither Raider nor Doc had much to say to Major Delaplane as they continued to wait for the troopers. There seemed little point in engaging in conversation that could only lead to arguing over the gamecock's obstinate stand. The passage of the sun through the heavens brought midafternoon. In six hours darkness would descend over the valley. In one hour, Raider estimated from what he could see going on below, Crazy Horse and his warriors would be leaving. If the reinforcements arrived before they did so, Raider had no doubt that Delaplane would order the attack.

"He won't wait ten seconds, Doc," whispered Raider, "lest we think he's backin' off his goddamn threat. Glory-hungry asshole! Look at him!"

"Keep it down, Rade. Don't antagonize him any more than you already have."

"*Me* antagonize *him?* You got it ass backwards."

"Something going on here I should be in on?" inquired a familiar voice behind them.

Lying on their bellies side by side, both turned their heads. Delaplane stood with his feet firmly planted, his twin ivory-handled Navy Colts holstered at his hips, riding crop in hand, and what looked like a pot on his head in place of his cap.

"Nothin' either o' us know 'bout," rejoined Raider. "What's that on your head, a chamber pot?"

"It's a battle helmet. Little invention of mine. It's patterned after what the knights of King Arthur used to wear to protect their brains, only heavier.'' He took it off and displayed it proudly. ''Half-inch cast iron. It'll stop a .45 slug at fifty yards.''

''If it doesn't, your head will.''

''Heft it.'' Delaplane handed it to Raider. It was so heavy he nearly dropped it. He pushed it into the major's midsection and Delaplane restored it to his head. It wobbled from side to side. It made him look even more ridiculous than he already did, reflected Raider sourly.

From down the hill behind them came a voice.

''They're acomin', Major!''

''And about time!'' rasped Delaplane.

Holding his battle helmet firmly on his head with one hand, he swaggered down the hill swinging his riding crop, his Colts bouncing at his hips.

''Asshole,'' murmured Raider. ''A bullet hit that thing, his head'll feel like a damn bell clapper. It'll rattle him deaf!''

A mounted battalion arrived, bringing the detachment's strength up to eight hundred guns. Arriving with the reinforcements was a tall, spare, white-haired full colonel. Delaplane introduced the two Pinkertons and Deputy Fales to Colonel Alfred Houston, commandant at Fort Edgerton. Hands were shaken all around.

''Sir,'' said Delaplane spiritedly, ''you're just in time. The men have been briefed and we're raring to go. We're going to mount up and ride down there and beard those red wretches in their filthy dens!''

Houston narrowed his eyes slightly and stared at his subordinate. ''You're not serious, Howard. From what I can see that's practically the entire Sioux nation down there.''

''Colonel . . .''

''I beg your pardon, Colonel,'' interposed Doc. ''May I say something?''

Houston nodded and listened while Doc explained and Delaplane sputtered, fidgeted, tried and tried again to interrupt, and finally resorted to raising his hand and waggling it like a schoolboy and generally making his presence obnoxious. At last he could no longer contain himself.

"Colonel! I say we get down there quick as we can. Not a moment to waste!"

"Hold your fire, Howard. What Mr. Weatherbee's saying makes sense to me. Our first concern is the lady and her well-being." He took off his gloves and glanced about. "It appears we have little choice but to bide our time. I suggest we all sit down and have a glass of wine. I've brought along one of my particular favorites, a Meursault. I do hope you're as fond of Meursault as I am, gentlemen."

"I can't speak for the others," said Doc, "but I find Meursault perfectly delightful."

Houston beamed. "Is that a fact, sir? Are you a connoisseur?"

"Hardly," responded Doc. "But who doesn't enjoy a crisp, fresh white Burgundy, and Meursault . . ." He bunched and bussed his fingertips in salute.

"Great Caesar's ghost!" snarled Delaplane. And throwing up his hands, he stalked away.

It was decided after the second glass that the Indians would not be leaving the valley through the narrow pass the hunting party Raider and Doc had followed had used. To the left, about a quarter of a mile distant, was a gap wide enough to accommodate a dozen ponies abreast. It appeared the most inviting way out.

As they sipped their wine the major gradually worked himself into a purple fury, insisting ad nauseum that once the main force had moved out of the valley they would be impossible to stop. They would spread out and wreak havoc for miles around. Delaplane had a distinct flair for the melodramatic, reflected Doc. He painted lurid pictures of horrendous bloodshed and destruction, burning, looting, scalping . . .

"Howard, Howard, Howard," interrupted Houston, holding up both hands in an effort to stem the verbal tide. "Calm down. I have no intention of letting them out of our sight."

Delaplane stopped short, his little pig eyes snapping in confusion. "You don't?"

"Certainly not. Here's how we'll work it. You will remain here with B Company. I'll take the main body and follow them. We'll cover their flanks, keep abreast of them, keep them in sight."

"But, sir, it'd be so much easier to fill that hole down there with continuous fire, pour in everything we've got. We can cork up the pass easy as pie, then come at them from the four points of the compass."

"Howard, that 'hole,' as you call it, has to be half the size of St. Louis. We could rush down there and chase around like jackrabbits until our ammunition gives out. What do we do then? They outnumber us five to one."

"They haven't got sixteen guns in the whole encampment."

Houston stood up, signaling an end to the discussion. "Assemble B Company back down the trail. Down by that big rock looks like a good spot. Keep two men up here as observers."

"And when the last mangy savage disappears over the brow of the hill, through the gap or wherever, we move on in!"

Houston shook his head emphatically. "Not until nightfall."

"But, sir!"

"That's an order, Howard."

"Yes, sir."

"Your assignment will be to rescue the lady. Your *only* assignment."

"Colonel . . ."

"Locate her, bring her out, and take her back to the fort. With as little bloodshed as necessary. Take her back or, if you prefer, send her back with a squad and you and the rest of your men rejoin us."

"Yes, sir."

"Tell Lieutenants Ormbsy and Fisher to get up here. Those of us leaving will be moving out shortly. Mr. Raider, Mr. Weatherbee, Mr. Fales, would you like to come along or remain here?"

Doc and Raider exchanged glances. "We'll stick here, Colonel, if you don' mind," said Raider.

"You do and you'll be under my command," piped Delaplane. "I'm in charge. What I say goes." Houston nodded.

"Understood," said Doc wearily.

A disturbing thought flashed across his mind. The best-laid plans of mice, men, and the military so often go awry. Such an outcome was practically guaranteed with a misfit like the major in charge.

CHAPTER SEVENTEEN

When Crazy Horse and his warriors rode out, Milena remained in her husband's lodge with two other squaws preparing food for the victors' triumphant return. At the same time, high up in the hills, Raider and Doc signaled Aaron to join them, and the three wandered off to talk privately. The major did not even see them leave, preoccupied as he was with preparing his men. No sooner had Colonel Houston and the main body of troops ridden out then Delaplane called for rifle inspection. Five hours later he was still at it.

"I don' like this, Doc," whispered Raider. "Major Shitheel's gonna screw things up to a fare-thee-well, jus' you watch. He'll get himself killed an' her too."

Doc nodded.

"He sure 'nough hates Injuns," commented Aaron. "Orders or no orders, he'll raise holy hob if we gets down thar an' any of 'em comes at us. An' they's sure to."

Again Doc nodded.

"Say somethin', Doc," said Raider.

"You two've said it all."

"Situation calls for drastic action."

"Rade . . ."

"Tap him on the helmet, lay him down 'hind a rock, an' let him sleep through the whole shindig."

"Forget it. Let me ask you a loaded question. I've never

155

seen so many tepees in any one spot in my life. How in the world do we go about finding her?''

"I already tol' you sixteen times, she'll be in Crazy Horse's.''

"And is there something special about his? Is it painted any special way, certain symbols?''

Raider shook his head.

"Isn't there anything? There has to be. The head man's house must show something to indicate his station.''

"If there is, I don' know it. I'm no Indian expert!''

"All right, all right, keep it down. When we get down there—''

"What makes you think Delaplane's gonna let us go down? This isn' our ball game anymore, or didn' you notice? From here on in it's Army doin's. Isn't that what the old man wanted? It's what he's got. Your friend the major is what he's got.'' He paused, spat, and muttered.

"We're getting involved with or without his permission,'' said Doc evenly.

"Now you're talkin'!'' Raider grinned and winked at Aaron. "Listen up real good, Mr. Fales. This is hist'ry bein' made here. This is the firs' time ever Doc Weatherbee's thrown out the book and played with his head. Firs' time an' prob'ly the last!''

"Oh, shut up.'' Doc scanned the sky. "It's going to be bright enough to read by, worse luck.''

"It's not gonna get any darker. Let's get goin'.''

Doc fastened him with a grim look and pulled his Winchester close.

"Lead the way.''

Darting from rock to rock, they reached the protection of a stand of cottonwoods. Raider raised his hand and signaling a halt.

"Keep down. It looks to me like there's no lodge set up closer than thirty or forty feet from the water. If we stick close to the river an' use the trees for cover . . .''

"What earthly good will that do us?'' rasped Doc.

"What's bitin' you?''

"I stepped in a puddle back there and got my foot wet halfway up to my knee."

"Clumsy asshole. Spill out your boot an' let's go."

"I asked you, what good will that do? She's inside his lodge, or at least close to it. How in heaven's name do we locate it? We've only got three thousand to choose from."

Raider thought a moment. Doc and Aaron studied him patiently.

"You two stick here."

"Rade . . ."

"I'm goin' scoutin'. Chances are his lodge is someplace near the center o' the camp. I think I can reco'nize the Oglalas' section if I spot it. His'd have to be there, right? Likely smack in the middle. I'll go have a look-see. I'll come back soon as I find the section, okay?"

"Be careful."

"Oh, hell yes, Doc. You think I'm stupid? You think I *want* another go-round with a damn panther? You think—"

"Just go, go!"

Luck was with Raider. Most of the braves who had remained behind—as well as the old men, the children, and the squaws—had, with the onset of darkness, abandoned the dying cook fires and removed themselves to their lodges. Luck stayed with him, and he located the Oglalas' camp with surprising ease: He recognized it by the ten pins above and below the door flaps, fewer than other tribes' lodges, and by the peculiar arrangement of the pot sticks over the cook fire.

Luck was still with him when he spotted the lodge of Crazy Horse. It had to be it, he thought triumphantly. He marked its location in line with a large willow standing forty feet away, then made his way back to where Doc and Aaron waited.

"Found it."

Doc's tone of voice in response was understandably skeptical. "Just like that."

"Easy as a sneeze. It's got to be it. There's a sacred tree smack in front o' it, painted all different colors. They musta held a Sun Dance 'fore they pulled out, the scarlet blanket test, the whole ritual.''

"Let's go."

"Hold it. We don' all three got to go. Let's work it in a relay. You, Doc, stick here. Mr. Fales, you get over to the foothills. By the time I get back here with her I'll be all outta breath. You, Doc, carry her to him. He'll—''

"What are you talking about, 'carry her'? She can walk, can't she?''

"She can, but she may not want to." Raider held up two fingers flush against one another. "Along 'bout now it wouldn' surprise me none if she an' him was that close. I'll likely have to put out her lamp to get her outta there without her kickin' up a fuss.''

"I can't believe that, Rade. I can't believe any white woman would willingly stay with Indians.''

"I can't help what you can't believe. That's the lay o' the cards, Doc. Crazy Horse had his eye on her back when. Only reason he never came near her was accounta Black Shawl. Now that she's dead . . .''

"All right, all right. Aaron, get back to the base of the hills and wait for us. Go and get her, Rade, but for heaven's sakes, whatever you do, don't start shooting.''

"Tell that to Delaplane. He's the one we gotta hold our breaths on. Whatever *you* do, don' get antsy if I'm not back with her in five minutes. Don' come lookin', for chrissakes. I can handle it.''

"Let's hope."

Raider fled, making his way back dodging from tree to tree. Reaching the Oglalas' location, he moved away from the river from tepee to tepee toward Crazy Horse's. He had come within sight of it and had crouched behind the sacred tree, getting ready to make a dash for the open flap, when he heard a soft step behind him. Pivoting on his heel and lifting his head, he lunged to one side—just in time to avoid a tomahawk coming straight down at him. Grabbing a leg as his knees hit, Raider pulled his attacker down. The tomahawk slipped from the brave's grasp as he fell. They scuffled briefly. The brave got hold of him by the throat, but as the two of them rolled over, Raider broke the hold easily and, freeing his right arm, smashed the brave hard on the side of the head. Moaning softly, the brave went limp. Raider got to his feet and glanced warily about. It seemed that the incident had gone unnoticed by any of the other Indians. Raider sighed his relief and, scurrying to the door flap, burst inside.

The lodge was empty.

"Son of a bitch, wouldn't you know . . ."

Sneaking back outside, he retrieved the tomahawk and shoved it through his belt. Then he pulled the unconscious brave inside and then moved to the side of the open flap. Going to his knees, the heel of his hand on his gun, he waited.

He counted the seconds to five minutes when suddenly a scream ripped the silence. Then came shots, shouting, and the sound of galloping.

"Delaplane . . . The stupid bastard!"

It was not unexpected. What was was Milena's absence from the tepee. It was Crazy Horse's, he was sure. She should have been there, but she wasn't. Now, with all hell breaking loose, she might not show up at all, he thought gloomily. What a lousy break! If only the gamecock could have held off another three minutes. If only he'd had sense enough to sneak in, instead of barreling in like a tornado and rousing the whole camp.

"Fuckin' moron!"

Outside, the tumult continued. He was preparing to sneak a quick look when in she stumbled. At the sight of him, she gasped.

"You!"

"Who you expectin', Nicky?"

She started back out, but he grabbed her by the wrist and pulled her down hard. The unconscious brave groaned, raising himself on his elbow, his hand going to his forehead. Raider pulled her over to the other side of the fire circle and, reaching across, delivered a hard right hand to the awakener's jaw, putting him back to sleep.

"I am not coming with you," she rasped. "I AM NOT!"

"Milena . . ."

"You cannot make me. My place is here, I am staying."

"You're comin' noisy, you're comin' quiet, whichever you like, but you're comin'."

She wrenched free and flung herself against a pile of buffalo robes, digging into them, pulling out a knife.

"Oh, for chrissakes . . ."

"Stay away from me. I will cut your heart out!"

She lunged at him. He sidestepped, avoiding the thrust, again grabbing her wrist. She screamed in pain. The knife fell into the fire circle. He knocked her cold, hitting her squarely on the jaw, twisting her head so severely that for an instant he was afraid her neck had snapped.

She lay still, her body absurdly contorted. Gingerly, carefully, he tested her head on her neck. He had not broken her neck, but she would show a fair-sized bruise to the right of the point of her chin. He studied her beautiful face by the dim light of the open flap and sighed. Then he sneaked a look outside. Delaplane and his men had poured down the hill, fanning out across the valley, stampeding through the tepees, slashing and firing at everything that moved. They had caught the camp by surprise, but now the braves had armed themselves and were fighting back. Raider cast a quick look to his left through the tepees to the trees and the river hidden in shadow beyond. If he could make it to the bank he would be clear of the battleground and his chances of getting up the line of trees to where Doc waited would be very good.

Raider retrieved the knife from the hot coals, burning his fingers as he did so. He went to the back wall and cut a long vertical slash through it, pulling the hides apart. Anyone coming in after they left might be fooled into thinking he'd taken the rear way out. Ridding himself of the tomahawk, he shoved the knife in his belt in place of it. Then he dragged Milena outside by the heels. A shot sang by, piercing the lodge less than six inches above his head. Crouching, he spun about. A wild shot, he decided. Nobody beyond the sacred tree—the direction the shot had come from—could possibly

see him against the dark background of the tepee. He slung
Milena over his shoulder like a sack of feed and, staying low,
duck-waddled toward the next tepee. To his right he could see
darkened figures, ten or a dozen dismounted cavalrymen and
an equal number of braves battling it out hand to hand with
sabers, pistols, lances, knives, and tomahawks. The screams
of the wounded and dying filled the night.

Doc watched the attack in stunned disbelief, then looked
anxiously down the way Raider had gone. He began moving
slowly in that direction. He ventured a few steps, reached a
tree, and paused. The water burbled softly through the darkness.
Delaplane was spreading his men all through the camp. It was
a reckless ploy that begged disaster, mused Doc. Thinning
their ranks so would isolate them, rendering them prime
targets for the defenders who, even with the vast majority of
warriors absent, unquestionably outnumbered the troopers.
Company B would be wiped out.

And yet how else could the major have handled it? Houston's
orders were to rescue the queen. No suggestions how to go
about doing so. That was for the major to decide.

How would he himself have gone about it? Perhaps attempt
to draw the bulk of the braves remaining behind away from
the lodges with some kind of diversion? And if it worked,
send in a handful of resourceful, experienced men to find her?
Had the major considered this, he wondered, or any other
alternative? After all, the idea was to get her out alive, which
had to mean with the least possible risk. Judging from the
uproar, Delaplane was studiously ignoring that aspect of the
thing. Perhaps he thought deliberately turning the camp upside down would be his best bet. Perhaps he actually believed
that the few men he had at his disposal were enough to wipe
out the defenders, and that rushing in and surprising them as
he had was all the edge he needed.

It was hard to know what went on in that mind. He
certainly didn't give the impression of enviable intelligence.
He was rash, stubborn, petty, and outrageously opinionated.
And, unfortunately, he was in sole command. He hadn't the

vaguest idea of his enemy's strength, and yet here they sat, occupying a space roughly the size of St. Louis, as Colonel Houston had observed. And he, Howard, had barreled.

Amazing, thought Doc. Such muddle-headed thinking, such rashness characterized so many forays against the Indians. White vanity simply refused to acknowledge red superiority in any respect. Arrogant and stupid officers of every rank consistently ignored the Indians' attributes: their familiarity with the terrain, their incredible adaptability, their resourcefulness, ruggedness, stamina, intelligence, and the fact that they were fighting for their lives. It was curious, even fascinating. Logic insisted that their so frequently proven ability to match firearms with primitive bow and arrow would oblige the military to take them seriously as an enemy. Too few officers did.

How Delaplane proposed to find the queen and rescue her in the midst of battle was beyond Doc. Hopefully, Raider had already found her and was now on his way back.

Doc squinted through the trees upriver. There was no sign of him. Closing his ears to the steady crackle of gunfire, the screaming and cursing to his left, he got out his watch and held it up, angling the face to catch a shaft of blue light conveniently offered by the moon. Nearly eleven minutes had passed since Raider's departure. What was delaying him? Where were they?

He's got her, Doc thought. He must by now. But can he get out of there?

Raider was trying. He slunk stealthily between two darkened tepees, Milena slung over his shoulder. The moon hung directly overhead, spotlighting them. He stopped short, swore, and dumped his burden as two braves rose up before him like phantoms from a grave, one wielding a saber, the other a tomahawk. They screamed and attacked. He caught the saber with a shot from the hip: The bullet pierced the brave's throat, stopping him cold and snapping him back as if he'd run full tilt into a tree limb. Gurgling horribly, his cry cut off, down he went. The tomahawk, following clumsily, tangled his legs in the dead man's. He teetered and fell. Flipping his gun in his hand, Raider smashed him in the temple and knocked him cold. He then retrieved the still unconscious Milena and, settling her on the other shoulder, struggled to his feet. He was just starting out again when, on the instant, in front of him and behind him, Indians and bluecoats were scuffling. Knives flashed. There was shooting, cursing. Easing Milena to the ground, Raider got out the knife and cut through the wall of the nearest tepee. He shoved her inside and dived in after her.

The fire threw a soft glow up the walls. The stink of tobacco filled the interior. The moon stared down the smoke hole. Seated cross-legged at the fire, bundled to the eyes in a buffalo robe, and looking as if he were carved from a single immense block of oak was Red Cloud. Raider recognized him instantly. Pipe in immobile hand, the old chief stared impassively at the fire, wholly ignoring the intrusion. Outside, the sounds of struggling, fighting, and dying went on. Raider moved to the open flap. He could see no one outside. He started out with Milena again, leaving Red Cloud as still as death, positioned and prepared to welcome its embrace, by the look of him. One last pipe, a final reflection on the state of man and his relevance to the Divine scheme of things, then off on the long and lonely journey to the happy hunting grounds.

Raider estimated the distance to the trees as a little more than a hundred yards, past twenty or thirty lodges. He was moving cautiously from one to the next and had covered half the way with surprising ease when out of the night two horses came thundering across his path. One caught an arrow in its withers, stumbled, and pitched its rider head over heels. The rider's head struck the ground and his neck snapped, the sound of a dry limb breaking. On rode the other without breaking stride, without looking back.

Blue smoke and the stink of cordite, the cries of the dying, the whooping and shouting and cursing of the still-to-die were all around him. Figures materialized, individual tableaus of combat cutting him off from the safety of the trees. And

Milena was getting heavier by the second, gradually reviving the dull pain in his bruised and still tender shoulder. He shifted her to the other shoulder. She moaned softly. Damn, he thought, what a time to wake up! He was reluctant to hit her again; doing so the first time had filled him with disgust. It was so easy, she was so vulnerable, but even if it was necessary—and it was—he felt a bully bastard doing it, his fist damaging, however slightly, that exquisite face.

He started. In his path was a young brave down on his knees, scalping a trooper: He set the point of his blade above the ear and, in almost a single motion, dug under the pate and swung around the front and the opposite side. The man screamed pitifully. Lifting the scalp with his free hand, the brave was about to detach it. Raider shot him in the face. The brave froze, the scalp uplifted, the knife poised, ready to slice. Blood spurted forth, flowering the center of his face, but, strangely, he did not fall. He stared out of his dead eyes at his killer, the blood spilling from his face. Then, very slowly, as if nudged by an invisible finger, over he toppled.

Raider bent over the trooper. His throat had been half cut. Blood seeped forth, crimsoning his tunic. He tried to speak but could not, his protesting scream the last sound out of him. He stared upward at Raider, his scalp dangling open. Raider closed it, closed his eyes, and laid him down gently.

Once again he started out.

Doc had moved up the line and was now debating whether or not to attempt to cross through the arena of death and destruction. By now a number of lodges were ablaze, going up like tinder, illuminating the grisly scene. He tightened his grip on the Winchester, cocked it, and crabbed forward.

Raider moved on until a voice called his name, freezing him in his tracks. He turned. It was Delaplane, standing spread-legged, a smoking pistol in each hand.

"Good boy, Raider. Is she okay?"

"Aces."

"Good, hand her over."

"Like hell."

"Give her here. That's an order!" Slowly he brought up both his six-guns.

"Order my ass, you stupid bastard!"

"Set her on the ground and back off with your hands up. I'll give you three seconds. One, two . . ."

Down came the barrel of the Winchester, striking Delaplane's helmet, setting it ringing and bobbling on his head. His knees gave way and he sank to the ground.

"Pick her up, Rade. Let's get out of here."

"You pick her up; she's heavy as hell. My damn shoulder's busted."

"Surely not both—"

"I already carried her a couple miles. Damn it, take over!"

"All right, all right, all right."

CHAPTER EIGHTEEN

The clicking of the rails and the gentle groaning of the car harmonized in a sprightly melody to Doc's ears. Relief over getting out of the valley alive and, miraculously, with Queen Milena unharmed and unblemished, save for the small bruise to the right of the point of her chin, filled his every fiber. Actually, it was something more powerful, more gratifying, longer lasting than relief: He felt like a man who had cheated a firing squad.

She sat between them dressed in a hoopless, straight cotton skirt decorated with tiny rosebuds, its bodice lined with canvas for extra strength and warmth. Long out of fashion in the East, out of fashion everywhere but on the frontier, the dress was a gift of Arabella Houston, Colonel Houston's eldest and prettiest daughter. Arabella had also given her a pair of sturdy button shoes and a slat bonnet, both of which Milena graciously accepted, and steadfastly refused to put on once out of the generous doner's sight.

The two Pinkertons and their companion had boarded the Chicago & Northwest Railway in Hot Springs, South Dakota, switching over to the Chicago, Burlington & Quincy in Crawford, Nebraska. And now, four days later, they were aboard the Union Pacific, with their eventual final destination New York City. A flurry of telegrams to and from Fort Edgerton had invested them with their final instructions.

Colonel Houston had tracked and eventually attacked and

dispersed the tribes within sight of Camp Holcomb, near Chalk Buttes, gaining the upper hand with help from the artillery units stationed there. Crazy Horse's allies scattered south into Nebraska and west into the mountains. Major Delaplane had returned from his escapade with only seven survivors of Company B. He complained of a ringing in his ears and the grandfather of all headaches. He confessed to not knowing "what had hit him." More importantly to Raider and Doc was the fact that he did not know "who."

They had sent Deputy Aaron Fales back to Pawnee City with a sealed letter for Marshal Tucker, written and signed by Doc, detailing Aaron's heroics and their gratitude for his help, adding that both would forever be in his debt.

Neither, at present, were in Queen Milena's. She made no secret as to her feelings over being rescued. "Kidnapped," she called it. For the first three days after their departure from Edgerton, she had refused to utter a single word. Raider was convinced that she would take the first opportunity to try and escape. Doc agreed. They took turns watching her like a hawk watches its field mouse dinner, prepared to pounce if she so much as set foot into the aisle of the car without declaring her intention to do so. While she slept, they shared guard duty in four-hour shifts.

The rough, barren tablelands of western Nebraska, broken with canyons, dotted with buttes, and dominated by bold, lofty ridges, gradually yielded to sand hills that rose in tiers, one above another, like miniature mountains.

They sat in silence, Milena continuing to seethe between them. Doc could almost hear her royal blood boiling. Let her stew, he thought. Let her burst a blood vessel after what she had put them through, Raider in particular. He would carry the scars of the panther's claws the rest of his days, and it would be weeks before his shoulder completely healed. What he had been put through elicited not a single spark of sympathy from her. Her previous fondness for him, an infatuation so consuming it had compelled her to kidnap him, had long since disappeared. She despised him. She couldn't look at him without her dark eyes firing, her jaw protruding defiantly, and her slender fingers going to work opening and closing. If she had been able to get her hands on anything even reasonably sharp, she would have cut his heart out, reflected Doc.

He reached into his vest pocket and brought out a little patch of buffalo hide. Unfolding it, he revealed her ring, the gold portion slightly melted, but the ruby and its ornamentation intact.

"This is yours."

She held out her open hand, glaring haughtily, mutely demanding he reach over to divest himself of the ring. She accepted it without looking at it, slipping it back on her finger.

Raider cleared his throat. "In case you're int'rested, your husban' and his maw are waitin' for us in New York."

"I am not in the least 'int'rested,' " she rejoined mockingly.

"As soon as we deliver you," added Doc, grinning to himself, pleased with the little turn of phrase that made her sound like a bale of wool, "you'll be boarding ship and heading home."

Raider chuckled and shook his head. "Old Nicky never did get to shoot his buffalo."

"King Nicholas!" she snapped irritably. "You will be respectful when you refer to him."

"Respectful, like you been. Loyal, devoted . . ."

"Spare me your ignorant views and crude English. I have had all I can tolerate of the two of you."

Again Raider chuckled. "Too bad. You still got 'nother four days to put up with us."

Sniffing disdainfully, she started to rise from her seat.

"What are you doing?" asked Doc.

"What does it look like? Which of you will follow me to the water closet this time? I do believe it's your turn, Raider."

She made his name sound like a rusty nail pulled from a board, thought Doc, amused.

"*Mr*. Raider to you, Millie."

"Animal! Upright swine! How dare you speak to me so! I shall have you—"

"Calm down, calm down."

Grasping her by the shoulder, he sat her thumping down.

"Rade, for heaven's sakes . . ."

"Take it easy, Doc. I got somethin' to say an' I'm sayin' it." Raider lowered his voice and bent his head slightly in an effort to keep what he was about to say from the ears of the passengers seated nearest to them. The car was less than a third full, but everyone's eyes had been on the three of them all the way from Northport Junction, where they had boarded.

"Missy," he growled, "you put me through a wringer with teeth in it. Nearly cashed me in sixteen diff'rent ways. That's sick'nin', but what really gripes is your stinkin' attitude. I was good 'nough for you back when. I was great, king o' the hill, back 'fore you crawled under Crazy Horse's blanket."

"Rade, that's enough."

"You serious? I'm jus' gettin' rollin'. . . . You call yourself a queen; you're not fit to rule a yard fulla hens. I've know a hundred whores who can out-lady you six ways from breakfast. You're the damn bottom o' the biggest heap in the barn. I feel downright sorry for Nicky, but even more sorry for you."

"You're ridiculous," she hissed. "Disgusting, contemptible."

"Let me tell you who I really feel sorry for: those people back to your home who got to bow down an' kiss the hem o' your skirt, an' call you Your Highness. That mus' be some four-bit country that can't find anybody better to be the queen than the likes o' you. I don' give that place six more years on the map with that silly-ass tin soldier an' a bum like you sittin' on the throne."

"Shut up, Rade!" rasped Doc. "You're making a spectacle of yourself!"

She shriveled him with a glare, got up, and started up the aisle. Doc was two steps behind her. Raider leaned back in his seat, shook his tired body into a reasonably comfortable position, and stared out at Nebraska passing by. There'd been so much more he wanted to say, he thought. Still, he'd made his point.

He smiled evilly, inviting and thoroughly enjoying the satisfaction settling in his stomach.

CHAPTER NINETEEN

The Pinkerton National Detective Agency's New York office at 66 Exchange Place was a dreary, dark-paneled cluster of low-ceilinged rooms stuffed with cheap furniture, barren of rugs, but, reflected Doc, as neat and orderly as a parsonage. It did, however, smell strongly of coal tar. George Bangs— tall, slender, affecting luxurious sideburns and a rather scruffy beard reminiscent of Allan Pinkerton's—sat at his desk in his shirt-sleeves, a two-foot stack of files in front of him. Behind him, a polished and gleaming Palladian window overlooked the heart of New York's financial district.

Bangs traced his ancestry back to the *Mayflower,* and he affected the cool, reserved air of a successful banker. He was the first man Allan Pinkerton had hired, and he had been his chief assistant in their Civil War operations. He had been with the agency twenty years. Doc liked him immediately after they were introduced by Bangs' elderly secretary. Liked him, that is, up until Bangs let it be known offhandedly that he was a Yale man. Having himself graduated from Harvard, Doc took an instantaneous dislike to the man—not so intense that it would prevent his working with him, not even a dislike, actually, more like sympathy for him for being so unfortunate as to have to attend a second-rate college. These earlier impressions shoved one another aside in reflection as Bangs rambled on to the two of them. Raider sat stiffly, his Stetson on his knee. He boasted a clean shave and a clear eye, and in

171

his belly was a Delmonico's steak. He looked oddly clad, every inch the country bumpkin in the big city that he was. Bangs gestured out the window in the direction of Battery Park and the Hudson River. Then he pointed to the right.

"Up there the docks begin. The *Great Eastern* should be putting in just about now. We could actually see it if we were next door. Some impressive sight. Today's Saturday. She'll be loaded and ready to leave Monday morning for Southampton. The royal party will be continuing on to Naples, and eventually to home port in Montenegro."

Raider shook his head. "Poor Nicky, all that fine hardware an' he never did get a buffalo."

"I understand he had planned to head back out from Kansas City, but a cable arrived from home. There's some sort of internal problem that requires him to get back to attend to."

Raider giggled. "I can't 'magine any problem he'd stick his two cents worth into that he'd help. Son of a bitch is 'bout as useful as a button on a cat's asshole."

Bangs stiffened and appeared mildly offended. Raider failed to notice. Doc did. Milena was right, he thought, amused: Raider *was* crude, but that didn't make his appraisal of His Highness, however colorful, inaccurate. Bangs was behaving oversensitively. Yale man, Yale snob, he thought. Recalling that he was known throughout the agency as a falling-down drunk sent a warm feeling through Doc's heart.

"I can't help sayin' I worry 'bout her," murmured Raider, offhandedly. "Bitch though she is."

"Her Highness?" Up went Bangs' right eyebrow. Tilting his head, he looked down his patrician nose at Raider. "You needn't worry. She's no longer your concern, old boy. Your job's finished. The agency was hired to protect the royal party on the buffalo hunt. Our responsibility terminated the minute they set foot on the train in Kansas City to come back here."

"All the same," said Raider, "I'm not relaxin' till their ship's back out to sea, an' I mean miles out. Anythin' happen to her now it'd give us a bigger black eye than we already got. She's trickier'n a snake; she can make anythin' happen."

Bangs chortled. "You're speaking from experience, of course."

Raider glowered at him.

"What a fascinating story it turned out," Bangs went on. "The newspapers are having a field day. It's knocked all that brouhaha over Irish home rule and the Baltimore whiskey frauds off the front pages of every paper from here to San Francisco. Too bad it makes you look like the bad guy, Raider. You should have let those reporters interview you, give them your side."

"Screw them. Buncha damn nosies. Whatever I tol' 'em, they'd screw it up. Always do."

"You're lucky the chief's willing to accept your word for what really happened out there, regarding who kidnapped who."

"Whom," corrected Doc.

"I don' know why he should," muttered Raider. "He hasn't asked me; I haven' tol' him. What makes me boil is the damn thing turns out no win either way. The truth, that she snatched me, makes me look like a horse's asshole."

"It certainly does," said Bangs, beaming. "Still, there's some consolation. You can say what you like about the old man, he's certainly rock-ribbed loyal to his people. Always has been. You can be grateful for that much."

Raider grunted. "Loyal an' six pounds o' fuckin' Bullard's Salve'll knit up my claw stripes an' fade the scars."

Bangs eyed Doc questioningly. "Does he always swear so, every other word out of his mouth?"

Doc frowned and shook his head. "I've never heard a cuss word out of him before. Not so much as darn or drat. Aren't you feeling well, Rade?"

"Shut up!"

A knock at the door. Bangs' secretary stuck her head in. Her face was like well-kneaded bread dough with her features flung into it almost willy-nilly, reflected Doc.

"Message, George. You and your visitors are invited to dinner with the royal family in their suite at the Astor this evening."

"How perfectly delightful."

"Messenger boy's waiting. Do I tell him you accept?"

"Tell him *we* don't!" burst out Raider. "Leastwise not us two. I've had my fill o' that bi . . . woman, an' if the ol' lady ever gets her hooks back into Doc, she'll never let go."

"We'll be there, Mrs. Maddox," said Bangs airily. He nodded, and she withdrew. "You two lotharios had better show. It wouldn't be very gracious not to. One can scarcely refuse a royal invitation, not and stay on the right side of Allan Pinkerton."

"Shit."

Raider got up, stretched, and wandered to the window.

"Seriously, Raider, what in the world is bothering you so?" Bangs asked.

"What do you think? How'd you like to have half the world thinkin' you're a kidnapper, an' the other half a horse's ass? You know somethin', Doc? I bet your two Secret Service buddies back in Kansas City still think it was me grabbed her."

"What do you care what they think? George is right. Allan Pinkerton's the only one who matters. Not Nicholas, not his mother. And the two of them know she instigated the whole thing. Of course they have to let her get away with it, sweep it under the rug for appearances' sake. Wipe the glum look off your face, Rade. Do you know what his whole trouble is, George?"

"Dyspepsia?"

"Brace yourself. The impossible has come to pass. My partner's in love."

"Why don' you shut your ass, Doc? You don' know what in hell you're talkin' about—as usual!"

"He is. She fell for him aboard the train, and he fell for her." Bangs gaped disbelievingly. "I mean it. No lie. That's exactly what happened. Then, when the Iversons grabbed her, and the Oglalas grabbed them both, everything started coming apart. Ah me, how right the old saying is: The course of true love never does run smoothly."

Raider lunged for him, swinging as he came, his right

glancing off Doc's shoulder. Bangs' posture chair tumbled to the floor. He shoved between them.

"Here, here, let's have none of that!"

Mrs. Maddox stuck her head in.

"It's nothing, nothing," said Bangs. "Just the chair. I slipped and fell over it."

She appraised him jaundicedly. "And what's the fight over—who's going to pick it up?"

CHAPTER TWENTY

Dinner at the Astor was served in a sumptuously decorated room boasting mirrors hung with brocaded old-rose satin, furniture rivaling that of the parlor car on the royal buffalo hunt train, and no fewer than four bronze and brass Gothic gas chandeliers for illumination. Everyone sat in handsome high-backed rosewood Gothic Revival chairs with finely carved detailing—pierced quatrefoils and elaborate finials—drawn to Raider's attention and painstakingly explained to him privately by his partner before sitting down.

They dined on bluepoint oysters, which Raider tasted, but declined to eat, a superb saddle of veal, vegetables—glazed carrots, tiny, succulent peas, huge mushrooms stuffed with cheese and herbs, and, for dessert, a selection of ices and trifles. Milena was not present, pleading, in His Highness's words, "a damned vicious headache."

Raider was relieved. Like Doc, he had accepted the royal invitation with reluctance; but again like Doc, he had actually been coerced into coming by George Bangs' threats and his lurid description of Allan Pinkerton's wrath and reprisal in some insidious form should either refuse to attend.

Doc sat nibbling nobly, tempted by everything but effectively reining in his voraciousness. As he joined in the meaningless chitchat he watched Raider out of the corner of his eye. He had never seen his partner so ill at ease, despite his undisguised relief at the queen's absence. He kept digging at

176

his collar with one finger to relieve the tautness of his tie, and again and again he cleared his throat nervously. He spilled fruit cup down his front and accidentally upset Queen Ernestine's goblet of wine. It was, decided Doc, the longest, most uncomfortable, most harrowing evening of the plowboy's life. And when it was over, shortly before ten o'clock, and the three of them had said their good-byes and were on their way down the corridor to the elevators, he presented the appearance of utter exhaustion.

Doc pitied him. His forced relationship with Milena w   an embarrassment to him, punishing his puritanical streak mercilessly. To add to his discomfort, he was lost amidst such surroundings, as out of place in New York City itself as a chicken in church. Allan Pinkerton could take him out of Arkansas, but neither he nor anyone else could take Arkansas out of Raider.

Late Sunday afternoon they went with George Bangs to say their final farewells to the royal family. Raider had never seen even a picture of the *Great Eastern,* and its size astonished him. It dwarfed every other vessel in sight, including the 3,670-ton *Adriatic* two berths away. Held in one piece by a reputed three million rivets, the *Great Eastern* was 693 feet long and 120 feet wide midships, with six masts and five funnels, more than any other ship ever built. A single power plant turned its twin fifty-eight-foot paddle wheels. A second engine powered her twenty-four-foot screw. Additional power was provided by 6,500 square yards of sail.

She carried twenty lifeboats and a pair of hundred-foot satellite steamers hanging from her sides. She had a capacity for fifteen thousand tons of coal bunkered around and over her ten boilers, the crew passing fore and aft through a six-foot iron tube buried under the mountain. She was a floating city, longer than the trough of the largest storm wave ever measured, and she rode so stably it was claimed that an army could be drilled on deck.

Recently she had been painted a ghostly white from stem to stern, which reduced by eight degrees the heat in her tanks, from which had spun the Atlantic cable. It lent her the appearance of an enormous iceberg.

Coal was being loaded as Raider, Doc, and George Bangs approached. They hurried up the gangway. Raider, in the rear, hung back, dreading the inevitable confrontation with Milena. He had been complaining about it all the way over from the office. Greeted by the first mate and ushered to the royal suite, they were welcomed at the door by Stefan. The man was as icy as Ernestine was warm, decided Doc, responding to his curt nod with a grim look. King Nicholas and Queen Ernestine greeted them effusively. Queen Milena, resplendent in a lovely white silk day dress with a strand of pearls at her throat and wearing a diamond tiara, nodded greeting but did not speak.

She looked tired, Raider thought, her eyes slightly reddened, her cheeks drawn and pale. She did not stand in her usual haughty manner, conveying the impression that everyone else present, including her husband, was less than ten inches tall. Instead, her shoulders slumped slightly. She looked as if she had just suffered a heartbreaking defeat of some sort. She also seemed nervous. Stefan brought wine, and small talk was contributed by everyone present—except Raider and Milena. King Nicholas presented both Raider and Doc with gifts: watch fobs inscribed with their names on one side and the royal crest in silver on the other. It was against agency rules for operatives to accept gifts from clients, but George Bangs considerately turned a blind eye to the gesture. The wine glasses were emptied, and the visitors exchanged farewells with their hosts and left.

Walking away from the gangway, still bringing up the rear, Raider turned for a last look at the ship. He saw Milena standing at the railing alone, the breeze whipping her dress, a flock of seagulls squawking insolently, wheeling, carving the sky high above her. She stared down at him. She did not wave. When their eyes met, she stiffened and turned away, walking down the deck and out of sight.

Slowly he turned his eyes forward and quickened his step to catch up with Doc and Bangs, who were waiting for him at the gate. Had he not turned his head immediately but had instead let his glance drift down the gangway to the stevedores loading coal, he might have spotted the two familiar faces in the group. They belonged to two big men with bull necks, powerful chests and shoulders, and arms and forearms revealing even rows of small scars.

CHAPTER TWENTY-ONE

The train lurched and clacked over the rails through the bleak, hilly countryside of northern Indiana. Raider woke from dozing, lifted his Stetson, and straightened in his seat. Doc was engrossed in examining his watch fob.

"This is a beautiful piece of work, Rade."

Raider grunted. "What do I need with a watch fob? Never carried a damn watch in my life. I know, it's the thought that counts. Know somethin'? Jus' between you an' me an' the fence post, not that I wanta sound ungrateful or anythin', but I think all three of 'em are crazy in the head."

Doc closed the box with a loud snap and restored it to his pocket. "Why do you say that?"

"They just are. The way they go 'long, makin' believe nothin' ever happened."

"We talked about that, Rade. They have to keep up appearances. It's . . . a royal obligation, actually. They also have to keep their emotional peace of mind, don't they?"

"That's phony. They can't just make believe it never happened."

"Of course they can't, but you can hardly blame them for trying to make the rest of the world believe it didn't. I give Ernestine and Nicholas credit. They've got class, Rade."

"Phony. How can Nicky an' her ever look each other in the eye again, knowin' what she did, how she carried on?"

"He doesn't care."

"Some husband."

"He can't afford the luxury of caring, if you will. And she's put it up on the shelf with a pink ribbon around it. Even Ernestine, as disappointed as she was that she came back, probably hasn't even mentioned it to her. She's simply ignoring it."

"Newspapers sure aren't."

"I doubt if any of them ever see a newspaper."

"Tickets, tickets . . ."

The conductor came at them, his walrus mustache stained around the mouth with what appeared to be tomato soup, his pale blue eyes squinting through his spectacles. Doc showed his I.D. card, and Raider, the temporary one given him by George Bangs. The conductor nodded.

"You boys going through to Chicago? Some doings, eh?"

"What doings?" asked Doc.

"The fire, didn't you hear?" They exchanged glances. "Burned up the whole city. Don't you read the papers?"

"The *whole* city?" asked Doc.

"Just about. Started Sunday night, nobody knows how, not yet. You know Chicago, it's like one great big cigar box. Went up like straw. Summer being so dry didn't help none. Last week alone there was twenty or thirty fires."

"Couldn't the firemen do anything?"

"They tried. Never had a chance. All tuckered out from fighting fires the week before. They say they had half their engines in for repairs, and their hoses was worn and leaky. Then too, a good stiff wind was coming off the lake all day Sunday. Surprised you didn't read about it in the papers. It's been in every one yesterday and today."

"Do you happen to know if Fifth Avenue was burned?"

"Mister, Fifth Avenue was in the heart of it. Started on De Koven Street and in half an hour the whole block was in flames. Wind blew it to the river and across it all the way to Lincoln Park and beyond."

"Then he's lost the offices and his house," said Doc to Raider.

"Everybody lost everything. You bet. Nearly twenty thousand buildings leveled. Lumber mills, bridges, even the courthouse.''

"Were many killed?" Doc asked.

"Hundreds, thousands, nobody seems to know the exact figure. Could be three or four thousand."

"Property damage must run into hundreds of millions."

"Half the city lost their homes and offices. All that wood, practically everything wood. Even the streets, paved with pine blocks." He shook his shaggy head. "Terrible thing, just awful."

"How about the Union Depot?"

"Fire never got that far." He moved on up the aisle. "Tickets, tickets . . ."

"You think the chief's all right?" asked Doc worriedly.

"Oh, hell yes, the whole lot's all right. Nobody'd be in the office on a Sunday."

"That's a break. I wonder where they set up temporary shop?"

"Cheapest hotel in town, where else?"

The first sight to greet their eyes upon leaving the train, even before they entered the station, was a large, intimidating poster:

Thieves & Burglars!

OFFICE OF

Pinkerton's Police

Orders are hereby given to the Captains, Lieutenants, Sergeants, and Men of Pinkerton's Preventive Police that they are in charge of the Burned District from Polk Street, from the River to the Lake and to the Chicago River. Any person stealing or seeking to steal any of the property in my charge, or attempt to break open the safes, as the men cannot make arrests at the present time, they

shall Kill the Persons by my orders, no Mercy
Shall be shown them, but Death shall be their
fate.

Allan Pinkerton

"Law and order stalk the city," chuckled Doc.

He bought a copy of Monday's *Evening Journal—Extra*.
Headlines screamed: "THE GREAT CALAMITY OF THE AGE!;
Chicago in Ashes!; Hundreds of Millions of Dollars' Worth
of Property Destroyed; The South, the North, and a Portion of
the West Divisions of the City in Ruins; All the Hotels,
Banks, Public Buildings, Newspaper Offices, and Great Business Blocks Swept Away."

"The conflagration still in progress," he read.

"Never mind, never mind, where do we start lookin'?"

They spotted a policeman, a round-and-red-faced, barrel-
bellied member of Chicago's finest, dozing against a wall,
and he informed them that the "Pinkerton De-tec-a-tif Agency"
had been burned out and was now located in the only building
untouched by the fire, the Lind Block, occupied by the Z. M.
Hall Wholesale Grocery firm, at the corner of Randolph and
Market streets. The building was on the shore of the Chicago
river and separated from the fire by an exceptionally wide
street.

They couldn't get a hansom, so they walked over. Edward
Wagner, the agency superintendent, looking as if he hadn't
slept in three nights, met them outside a glass door on which
a crude sign had been taped, identifying the temporary occupant.

"He's been waiting for you. I got your journal, Weatherbee.
Thanks for having the presence of mind to mail it from
Kansas City."

"No sense luggin' it to New York," said Raider.

"He must be pretty down about all this," said Doc, in a
tone calculated to test the turbulent waters.

"Down's not the word." Wagner shivered.

"I can imagine, losing the offices, his home . . ."

"That's not the half of it. He was just about to turn over

his Civil War files to the federal government. They were going to pay him $100,000.'' Raider whistled, Doc frowned, Wagner nodded. ''He got me out of bed around midnight Sunday and we came down to try to salvage the files, but it was impossible. The place was an inferno. He's still practically in a state of shock. You can go right in.''

''Thanks,'' said Raider dryly.

Allan Pinkerton sat at a desk so small it looked as if its previous user had been no older than nine. Bent over it, he was busily writing. The room was crammed with packing crates, and excelsior littered the floor. The windows were so grimy they dulled the rays of the sun trying to penetrate, forcing Pinkerton to squint as he wrote. After Raider closed the door behind them the only sound in the room for fully a minute was that of the chief's pen dipping and scratching, dipping and scratching.

Doc cleared his throat. Pinkerton started.

''Weatherbee, Raider . . .'' He extended his hand. They shook it in turn.

''Pull oop a crate. Sit, sit. No domn chairs, os you con plainly see. Well, well, well, well, well, so the grond escopade is ot on end ot lost, is it? With the twa oov you emorging oonscathed, I see.

He waggled a finger reprovingly. ''I was very ongry with you boys, verrrry oopset. Dinna speak. I've read your case journal since, hooever, ond I'm sotisfied with your explonations—moost oov your explonations, thot is. So the woman drogged you, Raider?''

''Yes.''

''How?''

''In my coffee.''

''Tsk, tsk, tsk. If you'd hod your wits aboot you ot the time you would hov caught her in the act, nae?''

Raider glowered. ''I wasn't lookin' for her to knock me out.''

''Thot's my point, you should hov been, mon, you really should hov. Olertnoss is the hallmark oov a guid professionol. Eyes ond ears, oll senses olert . . .''

"I beg to differ," interposed Doc. "He had no reason to suspect she'd try such a thing. Neither of us did. I would have been just as susceptible; so would you."

Pinkerton waved him silent. "Oll richt, oll richt, 'tis oll water oover the dom noo. Your job's doon. The agency's received payment in full for services rendored, ond the pesky lot are oon their way back to Mesoopootamia or wherever they coom from. Was it fairly uncoomfortable with the sovages?" he asked Raider, his tone tinged with sympathy.

"Picnic."

"You'd rother not talk aboot it, I take it. Os you wish, mon. Noo, let's get doon to bross tocks. We've a brond new ossignment for you two."

A knock sounded and the door opened. Wagner looked in. "Excuse me, Allan, a telegram's just arrived from George Bangs in New York."

"What's oon his mind?"

"The *Great Eastern* sailed—"

"Moonday morning, we know thot. By noo they're a thoosand miles oot to sea."

"*They* are, maybe. Queen Milena isn't." He waved the telegram. "She sneaked off the ship, George thinks in a spot called the Narrows. Picked up in the dark of night, probably by a tug or lighter."

"Dom the witch!"

Raider sighed and studied the ceiling. Doc shook his head.

"She's bock in the city? What does it say? Give it here, mon."

He snatched the telegram from him, hurriedly perusing it. "He doesn't say. Och. Oh well, she's nae oor responsibility onymore. Raider, Weatherbee, why would she do soch a dizzy thing? Ony ideas?"

"She's taken a likin' for the U.S.A., an' jus' doesn' wanna leave," said Raider.

"Vurry amusing, I dinna think." He crumpled the paper and tossed it in a corner. "Bother the woman. Pay no ottention to it, Edward. Leave oos aloon, if you dinna mind."

Wagner nodded and withdrew.

"Noo then, where were we? Och yes, your noo ossignmont. Gentlemon, I'm pleased to be able to inform you thot this one is richt oop your olley. It seems the Grond Duke Olexis oov Rooshia, son oov the Czar himself, hos orrived on oor shores for a guidwill tour, the coostumory shenanigans, dog ond pony show. Lavish cooverage by the press ond oll. Included in his itinerory will be a booffalo hoont. . . ."

Raider stirred, his face darkened, his jaw tightened. Slowly he began shaking his head. His own head down, talking into his tented fingers, Pinkerton failed to notice.

"He'll be hoonting the horned monsters in the vicinity oov North Plotte, Nebroska. General Phil Sheridon is orgonizing the hoont ond Lieutenont Colonel George Cooster will be oscorting the Grond Duke ond his suite."

"No buffalo hunts," said Raider flatly. "No more royalty, Grand Duke Whatsis, Archduke Whoozis. No private trains or Franchi Aristocrat rifles. No thanks."

"Dinna be hasty, mon."

"Dinna be shit! Give us a nice string o' bloody murders, a Wells Fargo holdup, shootin' galore, dead people up an' down the territories, but no buffaloes, bluestockin's, an' bo-fuckin'-hemians!"

Pinkerton studied him. The only sound was Raider's heavy breathing. Finally Pinkerton spoke.

"It was thot ooncomfortoble, was it?"

"It was a bitch on skates."

"Would you like to see his scars?" ventured Doc. "From a she-panther. She practically shredded him. Rade, unbutton your shirt."

"Noo, noo, noo, thot won't be necessory. You've made your point. Octually, I doobt if Sheridon ond Cooster will want coompony onyway. 'Twas joost a thought. I tell you what!" He slapped the desk with both hands and shot to his feet. "Why don't you two take the rest oov the day off. Give me time to find soomething for you. Relax, take a walk aroond the city . . ." He stopped short. "No, dinna do thot, it's too domned depressing. Joost go find yourselves soomething to amuse you the rest oov the day. Coom bock tomorrow ond I'll hov your ossignmont for you.''

He herded them out the door. They ambled down the hall and started down the stairs. At the first landing Raider stopped.

''He was sure in a rush to get rid o' us, wasn't he?''

''He was. I wonder why?''

In his office Allan Pinkerton stood at the door, his hand still on the knob. Slowly, carefully, he turned it. Sticking his head out, he looked up and down the hall. The coast clear, he snapped his fingers at Wagner in the office across the way, the door propped open.

''Pssst, Edward.''

Wagner came over to him. ''What?''

''They're gone?''

''They seem to be.''

''Guid. Get busy, get a wire off to Bongs. Tell him to contoct the *Great Eastorn* ot sea. Tell him to get thot King What's-his-name's authorization to start looking for Queen What's-her-name, the one thot joomped ship. Instrooct him to get oll the information he con so thot Raider ond Weatherbee con pick up ond follow through on it. Hurry, mon, there's nae time to lose!''

Author's note:

On page 169, in bawling out Queen Milena, Raider's words concerning Montenegro's future were unconsciously prophetic. The tiny country lasted not "six more years," but until April 1941. Following the collapse of Yugoslavia during the axis invasion of the Balkans, Montenegro was made into an Italian protectorate, whose "independence" was declared at Cettigne on July 12 of that year.